SPECIAL MESSAGE TO READERS

This book is published under the auspices of

THE ULVERSCROFT FOUNDATION

(registered charity No. 264873 UK)

Established in 1972 to provide funds for research, diagnosis and treatment of eye diseases. Examples of contributions made are: —

A Children's Assessment Unit at Moorfield's Hospital, London.

•

Twin operating theatres at the Western Ophthalmic Hospital, London.

•

A Chair of Ophthalmology at the Royal Australian College of Ophthalmologists.

•

The Ulverscroft Children's Eye Unit at the Great Ormond Street Hospital For Sick Children, London.

You can help further the work of the Foundation by making a donation or leaving a legacy. Every contribution, no matter how small, is received with gratitude. Please write for details to:

THE ULVERSCROFT FOUNDATION,
The Green, Bradgate Road, Anstey,
Leicester LE7 7FU, England.
Telephone: (0116) 236 4325

In Australia write to:

THE ULVERSCROFT FOUNDATION,
c/o The Royal Australian and New Zealand
College of Ophthalmologists,
94-98 Chalmers Street, Surry Hills,
N.S.W. 2010, Australia

THE HOUSE BY THE MERE

After the deaths of her husband and his secretary, Kate Byron was devastated to discover that, three years previously, they had had a son, Josh, together. Kate returns to Kenjarra, her childhood home, to sell her late father's estate. She meets opposition from handsome Nick Duvivier, the man charged with the restoration of the walled garden — but as the garden blossoms, so does their love. And as Kenjarra weaves its magic, Kate opens her arms to young Josh . . .

Books by Sylvia Broady
in the Linford Romance Library:

TO HAVE AND TO HOLD

SYLVIA BROADY

THE HOUSE BY THE MERE

Complete and Unabridged

LINFORD
Leicester

First published in Great Britain in 2003

First Linford Edition
published 2004

British Library CIP Data

Broady, Sylvia
The house by the mere.—
Large print ed.—
Linford romance library
1. Love stories
2. Large type books
I. Title
823.9′2 [F]

ISBN 1–84395–566–0

Published by
F. A. Thorpe (Publishing)
Anstey, Leicestershire

Set by Words & Graphics Ltd.
Anstey, Leicestershire
Printed and bound in Great Britain by
T. J. International Ltd., Padstow, Cornwall

This book is printed on acid-free paper

1

Kate Byron manoeuvred her car slowly along the narrow track sheltered by a leafy canopy. Between sturdy tree trunks, she caught a tantalising glimpse of Kenjarra Mere. As the trees thinned out she gasped with unexpected delight at the sheer beauty of the shimmering silver water basking in the early-morning hazy sunlight on this late August day.

Bringing her car to a halt, she leaned on the steering-wheel and let her gaze linger on the mere before turning her attention to the house by the mere — her childhood home, Kenjarra House. She was returning to her childhood home after an absence of twenty-five years. Now, memories of that terrible night flooded back and she shivered, when as a seven-year-old, her mother had pulled her from her warm bed to travel on a cold train to a strange town.

Now both her parents were dead, ironically within months of each other. Her mother did not believe in divorce, so neither parent had remarried. Kate wondered if her father had taken a mistress. It seemed to be the norm, she thought bitterly, acceptable for a man to have a wife and mistress, especially if the mistress gave the husband a child when the wife couldn't . . .

Kate's brown eyes filled with tears when she thought of the miscarriage she herself had suffered and the baby she had lost. She hadn't known of Vincent's mistress, not until she and Vincent, Kate's husband, had both been killed in a motorway pile-up, also that they had a three-year-old son, who mercifully survived the crash. The boy was an orphan in every sense of the word, having no other living relative.

After the boy came out of hospital, Kate, through her solicitor, agreed to finance the boy's upbringing with foster parents, but she wanted no contact with her late husband's love child. The last thing she wanted was to be reminded of Vincent and his mistress. Aunt Rosemary, her godmother, had agreed to visit the boy occasionally, to monitor his welfare.

Betrayal is an ugly word, especially when the man who betrays is your husband, someone you loved and trusted completely. Kate buried her face in her hands. Over and over in her mind she had tried to see where the marriage had gone wrong. Was she to blame for not seeing the signs? Now her husband was dead she knew she must try to move forward, but she had no idea how to. Perhaps she could once her late father's affairs were settled.

Feeling the need for fresh air, she stepped out of the car. A gentle breeze, wafting the fragrance of the wooded glade and the tangy smell of the mere, greeted her. The most wonderful feeling swept over her, confusing her. This feeling didn't fit in with what she had come here to do.

'You are trespassing,' a male voice boomed harshly, breaking into the peaceful atmosphere.

Startled, Kate spun round. Angry at the unwelcome intrusion, she glared at the man. He looked older than her thirty-two years, late thirties at a guess, tall, about six foot, athletic build with dark brown hair cut short and equally dark brown eyes. Wearing well-worn jeans and a T-shirt, his muscular, tanned arms glinted as he barred her way.

Determined not to be intimidated by this giant of a man, she demanded, 'More to the point, who are you?'

He seemed surprised by her forthright manner and answered, 'Nick Duvivier, gardener.'

So, she thought, this is the lofty Mr Duvivier who didn't want her to come here. It's no place for city dwellers he had told her solicitor. The anger had left her and she grinned mischievously.

'Good morning, Mr Duvivier. I'm

Kate Byron, owner of Kenjarra House and all of this.'

She waved a hand to embrace the surrounding woodland area, as he stepped back, his face expressionless.

'You were not expected until late afternoon.'

She wanted to say she didn't sleep much at nights since Vincent's death, but instead she said, 'I made an early start.'

He didn't comment, but his raised eyebrows seemed to ask, why?

'You'd better come up to the house.'

She would have preferred to linger in this idyllic setting, but now a member of staff knew she was here, she must make her presence known. She turned to her car but Nick Duvivier was already in the driving seat with the engine running. With as much dignity as she could muster, she slid into the passenger seat and looked straight ahead. There was something disturbing about Nick Duvivier, but she wasn't sure what.

Kenjarra House, bathed in shadows of the early morning, had an air of sadness about it. Kate shivered involuntarily, drawing her fleecy jacket closer. The car jerked to a standstill outside the front door entrance and the gardener jumped out and went to open the boot. She remained in her seat, staring up at the house. It wasn't a grand house but it was beautiful. Built in the early eighteenth century of mellow stone, its front door of panelled wood swung open. Kate saw a small, round woman framed in the doorway. She looked a pleasant woman, if she had been smiling. Kate felt cold, tired and hungry and her body ached for a long, hot soak in the bath and with this in mind she forced herself out of the car.

She held out her hand to the woman. 'I'm Kate Byron.'

The woman ignored it, turning her head to avoid eye contact with Kate, and said, 'I'm Maisie Fletcher. I used to be your late father's housekeeper. Now me and my husband are just care-takers.'

'Where's Wilf?' Nick Duvivier interrupted as he put down Kate's luggage he'd lifted from the car boot.

'He's out the back somewhere. Leave the luggage there and he'll bring it in later.'

'Might as well do it myself,' he said and without another word he picked up the cases and went into the house.

Kate followed Maisie into the long, high hall with soft green walls, where she admired a well-polished walnut table with a vase full of late summer colour. Maisie turned to Kate.

'Would you like to go straight up to your room and I'll bring you up a tray or would you prefer the dining-room?'

A knot formed inside Kate's stomach. She didn't want to go upstairs, not yet. She would have preferred the kitchen, but instead she replied that the dining-room would be fine.

Kate sat in the cold, impersonal dining-room, where a corner of the huge table had been set for one. She hadn't quite known what to expect when she arrived, but she hadn't expected to be made to feel so unwelcome. Her mixed emotions had veered from confusion, elation, anger, mischievousness and sadness and she was now drained of all energy, without a friend to confide in or to comfort her. She felt so lonely.

Her solicitor had suggested she employ professionals to value the house and contents for sale before putting the property on the market, but even though she hadn't seen her father for years, she couldn't bear the thought of strangers going through his belongings. It was the least she could do for him. Distressed after her husband's death, she had felt unable to deal with her father's funeral so she had left it to the services of a funeral parlour to carry out her father's instructions.

She drained her teacup and eating only one piece of toast, she rose from the table. A hot bath would help to ease her tension when she would have to consider where to start sorting out her father's house. She would like to be on friendly terms with Maisie and have her co-operation, but she wouldn't force the issue.

Leaving the drab room, she found herself standing at the foot of the staircase. Resting her hand on the mahogany newel she stared up at the repeating pattern of the barley-sugar balustrade leading to the rectangular gallery. Above the gallery was a circular cupola with a flat ceiling and windows to the skies. Her stomach knotted again and she closed her eyes, hearing in her mind her childhood screams as her mother bundled her down these very stairs.

Standing quite still, her breathing shallow, she broke out in a cold sweat. Dear God, she thought, give me strength. She wasn't a child any more. She was a grown woman. Opening her eyes, she took two very deep breaths to calm herself enough to begin the ascent up the stairs. Slowly, she reached the top and panicked again. She hoped Maisie hadn't put her in her old room. As luck had it, however, Maisie had put her in a bedroom on the other side of the house.

On entering the room, she went straight to the long window to gaze out on the magnificent view of Kenjarra Mere. Long before her father's time, the mere had once belonged to a titled family, Lord Kenjarra. Gradually the gambling of Lord Kenjarra's son lost the mere and the adjoining estate.

Turning from the window, she glanced round the room. Its walls were papered in faded blue, but the bed-spread was of fresh cream linen with beautifully-embroidered motifs of roses. The bed was unusual, with a solid, highly-polished wooden headboard and footboard curved in the shape of a swan. There was also a bedside table with a reading lamp, a huge wardrobe and matching dressing-table, but what delighted her was the small writing table and chair, placed to catch the light from the window.

She unpacked her case and then took off her travel-worn clothes and went into the bathroom next door to her room. The water struggled and gurgled, but at least it was hot as she lowered herself into the deep, porcelain bath scented with the oils of lavender and cedarwood. She lay soaking until the water turned tepid then after drying herself briskly on a soft, fluffy towel, she felt surprisingly refreshed and rather than resting on top of the bed, she dressed in jeans and a sweatshirt and decided to go for a walk.

Avoiding the kitchen, where she heard Maisie working, she borrowed a pair of wellingtons from the anteroom and slipped out through the side door.

From the kitchen window, Maisie saw Kate round the corner of the house and make her way to the path leading down to the mere. As she filled the saucepan with cold water, Maisie couldn't help noticing the slump of

Kate's shoulders, the thinness of her figure and instantly she felt guilty. She'd given her such a meagre breakfast and the lass had travelled far and through the night. As well as the death of her father, the lass had lost her husband in an accident. She must still be grieving and she, Maisie Fletcher, hadn't shown her an ounce of sympathy.

'My breakfast ready?' a voice growled behind her.

Maisie turned slowly round, her face grim.

'Hungry are you then, Wilf?'

He stared at his wife.

'What are you on about woman? Of course I'm hungry. I've been working though nobody appreciates me.'

He dropped heavily on to a chair at the table and picked up the morning newspaper and propped it against the marmalade jar. Maisie busied herself taking sizzling bacon from the pan and placing it between two thick slices of freshly-baked bread. She topped it with mushrooms and set it in front of Wilf, then, pouring two mugs of tea, she sat opposite him.

'I can't do it, Wilf.'

He didn't look at her but carried on munching his food and reading the newspaper.

'I can't ignore the lass.'

Now he did look up.

'Why not?' he spat out. 'She doesn't give a damn about us. How we are going to manage when she sells up? I've got five years to retirement and if I don't get another job you can kiss goodbye to our bungalow at Burtonsea. So think again, woman.'

He pushed back his chair and stomped from the kitchen. Maisie sighed deeply. She knew Wilf was right and it hurt her to see him so angry when usually he was a mild-mannered man, but all their dreams, their plans for a comfortable retirement had fallen apart with the death of Christopher Mansell, Kate's father.

Unaware of the affect her decision to sell was having on other people's lives,

Kate was walking through woodland and welcomed the peace and tranquillity. The day was warming up and reaching the edge of the mere, she breathed in the fresh, scented air. Observing through shaded eyes, Kate could see that this area fringing the mere was more natural, having retained its woodland in comparison with the far side of the lake.

'It's them boating people across the mere,' a voice echoed in the stillness.

Startled, thinking she was alone, Kate turned to see an old white-haired man sitting on a fallen tree trunk.

'You be Violet's girl then?'

At first she thought he had mistaken her for someone else then she realised he meant her late mother. She had been called Violet, though Kate could only remember her referred to as Mrs Mansell, except by Aunt Rosemary.

'Good morning,' she offered politely. 'You have the advantage over me. I am Violet Mansell's daughter, Kate Byron. Do I know you?'

He chuckled.

'Aye, lass, a long time ago. You were just a nipper, with long legs and long fair hair. You were a bonny girl, just like Violet. I'm Harry Leland. I used to be head gardener in the old days, though I still help out.'

'I'm sorry, but I don't remember you. In fact, there isn't anything I remember. I was so young when I left Kenjarra.'

She sat down on the log beside the old man and the nightmare of her last night at Kenjarra replayed again in her mind's eye. She had never told anyone of her fears, the shock of being snatched from her warm bed, her mother's hysterical sobs frightening her, making her cry, the journey on a cold train and an even colder railway station where they waited for a connection.

Her mother had taken a succession of live-in housekeeping positions in the Cambridgeshire area where Kate could be with her. Every day, Kate pleaded with her mother for them to return home to her daddy, but Violet was always adamant that they would never return to that man.

Kate stared at the mere now, seeing reeds poking up, their spikes tinged with grey and yellow, and multi-coloured dragonflies winged on the water's surface.

'An idyllic place,' she murmured aloud.

'Aye, you're right, but what will become of it when you sell up?' Harry retorted fiercely.

Surprised by his words she turned sharply to look at him.

'Nothing will happen to it, surely?'

'Bulldozers will move in. The boat club wants full access to the mere. They want another road in so they can have more berths, and that's only for starters. The old house will become a boozy den or worse still they'll pull it down and build one of them modern monstrosities.'

Once Harry was in full flow there was

no stopping him.

'And what about the gardens?'

Suddenly his words became too much for him to bear and he stopped as his eyes filled with tears.

'The gardens?'

She thought about the wide expanse of lawn and the old oak tree, the beautiful, wooded glade, home to small creatures of the wild, and the host of birds nesting in the trees and hedgerows.

Then in a soft voice, Harry said, 'This is where Dorinda drowned.'

'Dorinda?' she asked, wondering whom he was talking about.

'Dorinda Whitely, your mother's best friend.'

Then Harry looked at Kate with deep, glazed eyes and a shiver ran through her body.

2

Harry Leland continued talking in the same soft, far-away tone. Feeling an intruder, Kate shuffled uneasily beside him, but felt compelled to listen.

'Dorinda was the most beautiful lass you could imagine, with long, flowing black hair and eyes that shone like stars, so full of life, but wild with it. They say her mother was a gipsy woman, died giving birth to her. Her father, Ed Whitely, came to work on the estate and married one of the Wilson girls, Betty. Betty and Ed had a brood of kids and Betty brought up Dorinda as her own. A lovely family till tragedy struck.'

Harry's voice trailed off and he heaved himself up from the fallen tree, his old bones creaking as he leaned on his walking stick.

'Must be off. I've work to do.'

Kate watched, surprised at Harry's agility as he ambled away, cutting through the undergrowth and disappearing from view. Rising to her feet, she stood at the edge of the mere, peering into the dark, deep water. She shook herself, suddenly feeling very weary. The long journey from Cambridgeshire was finally catching up with her. Her legs brushed against the damp, springy grasses as she turned to retrace her steps through the woodland back to the unwelcoming house.

'Mrs Byron,' Maisie called as she went inside.

Kate had been hoping to slip unnoticed into the house. She couldn't face more unpleasantness from the woman. She just wanted to be alone.

'Yes?' she answered back.

Maisie flinched involuntarily.

'Mrs Byron, just to say that I'm cooking an early lunch. Half-past twelve suit you? I've set a place in the dining-room for you.'

It's so cold and unfriendly, Kate

thought as a vision of a warm kitchen appeared in her mind's eye.

'Thank you,' she replied.

Her steps were heavy as she ascended the staircase. Maybe somehow she could win Maisie over. She would welcome help with the unenviable task of sorting out her father's belongings, his clothes and such like, but she would have to go through his private papers and documents on her own. She wasn't looking forward to any of it.

Her father, Christopher Mansell, had been a stranger to her. When she had married Vincent, she had desperately wanted and needed her father, but now she felt nothing for Christopher Mansell. As far as she was concerned, he had abandoned her and her mother and the sooner she sold up, the quicker she could get on with the rest of her life.

She put her hand on the doorknob of her bedroom, and then stopped. Her future — what was it? Her hand trembled as she opened the door. As far as she could see, it was bleak.

Unable to rest, Kate tidied away her clothes and put a couple of paperbacks she'd bought at a motorway service station on the bedside table. Then she looked out of the window towards the mere and couldn't help wondering how the mysterious Dorinda had come to drown in those still waters.

Restless, Kate decided to wander downstairs and find her bearings in the house. She would ring Aunt Rosemary in the evening to let her know she had arrived safely. There was nothing else to tell. She could hardly say the natives were unfriendly because she didn't want to worry her aunt.

On reaching the bottom step of the staircase, she heard a scream wrench the air. Kate immediately ran in the direction of the kitchen where she found Maisie in a heap on the floor and a pan of potatoes scattered about. She was trying to raise herself on her elbow. Instantly, Kate kneeled beside her, unable to avoid the water spreading over the floor.

'Don't move. Let me check for any broken bones. Does it hurt anywhere?'

She remembered everything from her first aid course when she worked at the library.

'My ankle,' Maisie said and the pain in her grey face was obvious.

'What happened?'

'The pan handle gave way.'

After a quick check, Kate said, 'I don't think you have any broken bones, but your ankle looks as though it's badly sprained. It would be advisable to go to hospital for an X-ray.'

'I can't go now. I've the lunch to see to,' she wailed.

Noticing the shaking of Maisie's body, Kate didn't argue with her.

'First, let me get you up and make you comfortable,' she said, though it was going to be difficult on her own because Maisie was endowed with quite an ample figure.

'Let me help,' a strong male voice said.

Kate was very conscious of Nick Duvivier's nearness, breathing in his smell of the fresh outdoors. Nevertheless she was grateful for his appearance and help. They sat Maisie on a kitchen chair and Kate sponged the older woman's face with cool water bringing back some colour to her cheeks.

'Did the water from the pan catch you at all?'

'No, just the edge of my apron,' she replied.

Kate untied the strings of her apron and eased it off then she made Maisie a cup of hot, sweet tea. Gradually, the woman stopped shaking. Meanwhile Nick had gone to fetch Wilf who now came blundering in.

'You do too much, woman.'

But he was gentle with Maisie as he helped her on with her coat and out to the car.

'Shall I come with you?' Kate asked, hovering by the side of the car.

'I can take care of my wife,' Wilf grunted.

After watching the car disappear round the corner of the drive, Kate went back into the kitchen, where she was surprised to find Nick had gathered the scattered potatoes and put them in the waste bin and was now mopping the wet quarry-tiled floor. Somehow he hadn't struck her as the domestic type, but then she didn't know him and she wasn't likely to.

Skirting round the wet floor and avoiding Nick, she made her way towards the ancient cooker to check on the rest of the food. Opening the oven door she found a casserole simmering. Lifting the lid of the dish a rich aroma of succulent juice filled her nostrils. She picked up a spoon and gave it a stir, resisting the temptation to taste it.

'That smells good,' Nick said close to her ear.

Startled, the lid of the dish wriggled precariously as the oven cloth slipped.

'Careful!'

He leaned across her, rescuing the

cloth and the dish then he firmly shut the oven door. Taking hold of Kate's arm he helped her to her feet.

'We don't want another accident,' he said.

She shook her arm free from his grasp.

'It was your fault creeping up on me,' she replied heatedly.

He stepped back.

'Why on earth did you have to come here if you feel so irritated by it?'

For one unbelievable moment she thought she was going to cry and her voice trembled as she replied, 'To get to know my father.'

She spun round then and fled the kitchen through the side door and out into the garden. Stumbling, she sank down on to the small flight of stone steps leading down to the lawn. Her reply to Nick had stunned her. How could she get to know her father? He was dead. It was too late.

She should have made an effort to contact him before he had died and not be persuaded by her mother's vindictive tongue. Now she would never know him. She shivered as her wet jeans clung to her legs. She'd made a terrible mistake in returning to Kenjarra. If she weren't so tired she would leave right now.

'Mrs Byron, Kate,' Nick was calling softly.

She glanced over her shoulder and saw him approaching with two steaming mugs and a car blanket slung across his shoulder. He thrust a mug of tea into her hands and placed the blanket gently about her shoulders. Cupping the mug, she sipped the hot, sweet liquid. If she hadn't been feeling so miserable she would have laughed. He had given her hot, sweet tea for shock just like she had given Maisie. The blanket was warm and comforting and she buried into it as Nick stood awkwardly by her side.

'Look, I'm sorry. I didn't mean to upset you.'

Then he sat down on the steps

thinking how sad she looked. Earlier he had seen her vibrant spark of life but now it was extinguished. Was he responsible for that? He sighed heavily. Each day brought a new problem and he could see no end in sight.

Kate glanced at him.

'You don't have to worry. I'll be gone by morning.'

He rose to his feet and said icily, 'I don't think your father would have approved of you running away.'

She glared at him.

'Isn't that what you all want?'

'Christopher Mansell was a proud man and he was also my friend. I think you should do the right thing by him,' he said and with that he turned and strode away from her.

Her eyes followed his disappearing figure and then slowly she pulled herself up. Collecting the two empty mugs and folding the blanket over her arm, she marched back into the kitchen. She wasn't going to give in easily. Surveying the kitchen, the first thing she must do was to salvage the lunch, after changing out of her wet jeans.

About an hour later, Kate heard a car drive up and Maisie hobbled into the kitchen followed by an attentive Wilf who seated her at the kitchen table. Maisie's eyes lit up with surprise and she gasped with delight. The table was set for four people with a jug of freshly-squeezed orange juice, tureens of piping hot of vegetables and Kate was placing the casserole dish in the centre of the table.

'How's the ankle, Maisie?' Kate asked, concerned.

'Just a sprain, but I need to rest it for a couple of days.'

'That's not a problem. I'm here so you can take it easy.'

'Are you sure?' an anxious Maisie asked.

' 'Course she's sure,' Wilf interjected gruffly. 'And I'm starving.'

Nick came into the kitchen and began talking to the couple. Kate avoided his eyes and busied herself by dishing up the casserole.

'Well, I never,' Maisie exclaimed. 'I never thought I'd be sitting down to my lunch today.'

She beamed at Kate, who felt the good factor fill her mind and body. As she looked round the table happy to see everybody tucking in, Nick caught her eye and winked at her, but she ignored him.

Later that evening, Kate telephoned her Aunt Rosemary.

'How are you settling, dear?'

Kate played the light-hearted part, making her aunt laugh as she relayed the saga of the pan of potatoes and Nick cleaning up the kitchen, then how she would be helping in the kitchen until Maisie was well enough to cope. But Kate was careful to leave out the unpleasant happenings since her arrival at Kenjarra.

* * *

Kate studied her face in the dressing-table mirror. She hadn't worn make-up for days, not since arriving at Kenjarra House a week ago, yet her skin was silky and her cheeks shone with a rosy hue. Brushing her thick shoulder-length hair back into a sleek style she hurried from her bedroom dressed casual in jeans and a sweatshirt. Today she was definitely going to make a start and go through her father's possessions, though she wasn't looking forward to doing it, not sure what she would find.

To her relief, Maisie, now recovered from her ankle injury, volunteered to help by arranging for one of the charity shops to collect any spare clothing after Wilf and Harry Leland had taken their pick. Nick Duvivier declined the offer of anything.

The room that had been her father's was at the front of the house at the end of the corridor and to reach it she had to pass her old room. Its door was shut tight and she felt no temptation to open it to dredge up the painful, confused memories of her last night spent in that room.

Standing on the threshold of Christopher Mansell's room, an overwhelming sadness filled Kate and for the first time in many years she cried for the father she had lost. She flung herself on to the bed face down, sinking into the feathery duvet. She wept, not only for Christopher but for Vincent, her erring husband, who had so cruelly betrayed her. She didn't hear the soft footsteps of Maisie come into the room and then retreat.

About twenty minutes later, Kate went into the adjoining bathroom to splash cold water on her face. She felt a little better but still sad. As she came out of the bathroom she met Maisie, carrying two mugs of steaming coffee.

'Milk, no sugar? Have I got it right?' she chirped.

Appalled by Kate's sad appearance, she kept up a light banter, giving the girl time to compose herself. Maisie made a silent vow that, come what may, she intended to help Kate. Wilf would understand, eventually.

On entering the bedroom again, Kate noticed it contained only minimal furniture and fittings. Besides the huge, brass bed, there was an Edwardian-styled wardrobe and tall boy, a small bedside table and two upright chairs. There was nothing to suggest that once her mother and father had shared this bedroom, no feminine touches of any description, past or present. Off the bedroom was a small dressing-room with an oak bureau where her father kept his private documents. She fingered the key in her pocket and turned away.

Her coffee mug in her hand, Kate went over to the window and looked down on to the driveway and a bed of pink roses edged in by deep blue lavender. The scent of the flowers drifted up through the open window. She was aware of Maisie by her elbow.

'Your father loved flowers, in fact over these last few years gardening became his obsession.'

Kate glanced over her shoulder at the older woman.

'Had you worked for my father long?'

'Twelve years, when Wilf was made redundant from the farm. This job was a godsend because we had a place to live. Ever since then, we've been saving up for a bungalow for when Wilf retires. But now?'

Maisie's voice wobbled.

Kate turned round surprised to see tears glistening in Maisie's eyes.

'What's wrong?'

'It's not right for me to say.'

Kate's head began to hammer. She wasn't up to riddles, but the situation, whatever that was, called for tact and she liked the woman.

'Maisie, tell me what's bothering you,' she asked.

Maisie moved away, rearranging the tidy bedside table.

'Me and Wilf won't be able to buy a bungalow now, not with us being out of work.'

'But you are both working!'

'What happens when you sell up? What will become of us?'

Head bowed, she gripped the edge of the table with both hands. She had one more thing to say. Kate hadn't moved, but now she understood the attitude of Maisie, Wilf, Harry and Nick. They were fearful for their futures, just like she was.

From what seemed a long way off Maisie mumbled, 'You see, we all thought Mr Mansell would leave everything to Nick. We didn't know he had a daughter. He never talked about you!'

The words hung ominously in the air.

3

The room whizzed like a carousel, its music off key, jarring. Kate put her hands to her head, waiting for the movement within her to stop. When it did she released her hands and stared at Maisie and when she spoke, her voice was barely audible.

'You must all hate me so very much.'

Maisie flustered. She'd said too much.

'It's not your fault, lass. It's just . . . '

She didn't know what else to say. Wringing her hands, she made to the door, to escape.

'I must go. I've lunch to prepare.'

Alone, Kate turned back to the window to stare unseeingly out on the now drizzly landscape. So wrapped up in her own world of sorrow and heartache, she had given no regard for the people who had been her father's employees, and for that she felt ashamed. She just assumed that whoever bought Kenjarra and its land would keep on the existing staff.

Then the words of Harry Leland came to mind about the house being turned into a residential home and the land cleared to make way for the yachting club. Now she wasn't sure what to do. Her thoughts muddled, she went through into the little dressing-room-cum-studio and sat down at her father's bureau.

Tracing her fingers over the cool, polished oak, she could see years of care gone into its maintenance. She glanced up, noticing on top of the bureau the silver-framed photograph of a young man in RAF uniform. Although his face was unsmiling, his eyes twinkled and she knew instantly it was her father. She had never seen a photo of him before and her difficulty, as a child, was to conjure him up in her mind's eye. Whenever Kate had asked her mother what he looked like she always evaded the answer.

'A child shouldn't grow up without its father,' Kate murmured softly.

Then a thought jumped into her head. Vincent's child, a little boy, would never know his parents — but he had good foster parents and was well taken care of.

She fumbled in the pocket of her jeans for the bureau key. It was now or never. She turned the key, listening to the spring of the catch. Hesitating for a second she opened it and gently let down the writing flap. It was of tarnished brown inlay leather and she saw a small burn mark, like from the bowl of a hot pipe put down in haste. Crammed in the pigeonhole compartments were receipts, some faded. So her father had been a hoarder!

Tucked in one corner was a green leather-bound book. She reached for it and squinted at the faded, embossed title on the spine, **The Golden Treasury by F T Palgrave**. There was a bookmark, in cross-stitch, the type a child makes at school.

Her heart gave a great lurch. Had she made it? A picture long hidden in the recesses of her mind flashed into her head, the shadowy figure of her father meeting her at the school gate and hot in her grubby, little hands she clutched the bookmark. There were tears in her father's eyes as she gave it to him. He wasn't a man given to showing emotion and she thought it strange at the time. Now she knew why, or did she?

She opened the book at the place he'd marked, a poem by William Wordsworth, *Written In Early Spring*. Kate began to read the beautiful but sad words. When she finished she was crying tears of pain for her late father. Deeply moved, she held the book of verse in her hands for a long time before replacing it and locking the bureau. Rising from the chair, she gave a heavy sigh, not realising that looking through her father's possessions would drain her energy so. Her head ached and she needed fresh air.

It was still raining as she made her way down to the mere, but her thoughts were in such a whirl that she didn't notice the weather. On reaching the water's edge, she sat down on the log and gazed out across the calm stretch of water. It was so peaceful here. She thought of her father — had he ever sat here? Drawing on the tranquillity, her mind cleared. Once she had been through the documents in the bureau and seen her father's solicitor, she would make an appointment to see the estate agent.

Kenjarra is a family home, she told herself, and it needs the laughter of children to bring it to life. She would stress to the agent that she would only consider couples with children, who were prepared to keep on the existing staff. Then a little voice in her head butted into her thoughts — why don't you keep Kenjarra? Aloud she answered, 'But I'm now a single woman and childless. What would I want with such a house?'

She wasn't even going to consider it, she thought as she walked back to the house through the woods. She would miss Kenjarra, however, even though she only had been here a short time.

Later, at supper, she chatted aimlessly to Maisie, as if their earlier conversation hadn't taken place. Wilf was silent as usual and of Nick there was no sign.

As Kate helped to clear the table, there was a knock at the door.

A female, breezy voice called, 'It's only me,' and a vivacious redhead entered the kitchen, dressed in a trendy blue jogging suit and matching trainers, carrying a bottle of wine.

'Hi, thought I'd better show my face and be neighbourly,' she addressed Kate. 'I'm Denise Morgan. I live in the cottage down the lane with my brood.'

She shook Kate's outstretched hand. Kate took an instant liking to this woman, so full of life, and she eyed the wine. Not a drop had touched her lips since Vincent's death, a sort of penance she'd installed on herself.

Wilf had sloped off and Maisie had finished putting the dishes away and was hanging up her apron.

'See you in the morning, Kate,' she said and nodded to Denise as she went off down the narrow corridor to her sitting-room.

Denise tossed her head.

'Maisie doesn't approve of drink. I think Wilf was too fond of the whisky at one time.'

Kate reached for two glasses from the cupboard and set them down on the table while Denise opened the bottle.

'I'm afraid it's only supermarket special offer, but we're on a tight budget with buying our cottage. We finally persuaded Mr Mansell to sell and we did it within the nick of time before he died.'

She stopped on seeing Kate's face twitch.

'Oh, no! I'm sorry. That was thoughtless of me.'

She quickly poured the wine and took a gulp.

'Your dad was a nice man. Reserved, he was, but he loved talking about his gardens. Funny though, he never talked about you.'

She stared across at Kate.

'My parents separated when I was a young girl and I lived with my mother until I married.'

'You're married? Have you children?'

'I'm a widow and I've no children.'

'Gosh, I'm sorry. You're having it rough. I tell you what, whenever you feel in need of boisterous company, come to the cottage any time. In fact, come tomorrow night for supper. Frank's playing in a darts tournament and the kids will be in bed. I'd welcome the company.'

'Will I get to see the children?'

Kate suddenly had an overwhelming desire to cuddle a child.

'Sure. Come about seven. They're little cherubs after a bath.'

Kate gave a girlish giggle. The wine

was having a lovely warm effect on her mind and body!

For the first time since Vincent's death, Kate slept right through the night and in the morning woke up feeling energetic. Was it the wine or the good company of Denise last night? Both, she reckoned, and there was the evening to look forward to.

Armed with a bottle of red wine, Kate set off to Denise's cottage. She was looking forward to meeting the children. A sudden rush of sadness filled her. If only she had gone full term with her baby, then perhaps Vincent would not have felt the need to take a mistress and have her child, and he might still be alive. A deep sigh escaped her lips. She must stop dwelling on the past and make a determined effort to think positive.

She was looking forward to a relaxing evening and chatting with Denise. She wanted to ask her if she knew anything about the mysterious Dorinda who had drowned in Kenjarra

Mere. But on reaching the cottage, a far from idyllic scene greeted her. Denise was standing on the doorstep of the whitewashed cottage with her outdoor clothes on.

'Thank goodness you've come. My mum has been rushed into the cottage hospital and Frank's out. Could I leave the children with you?'

'Why, yes.'

'Thanks,' Denise exclaimed and rushed to her car.

In no time at all, she had sped away. For a moment Kate remained motionless then the sound of children squabbling drew her into the cottage. There, in the well-lit sitting-room, wrestling on a rug in front of a television set, were one redheaded boy of five and a dark-haired girl of around seven.

'Give it back to me,' the girl demanded as she tried to snatch back the TV remote control.

It slipped from the boy's hand and in a flash Kate picked it up and zapped off the TV. Two startled pairs of eyes gaped at her.

'Hello,' she said. 'I'm Kate.'

She crouched down to their height.

'What's your names?'

The girl answered, 'He's Liam and I'm Holly. Are you our baby-sitter?'

'Yes, I suppose I am.'

Holly sat up, cross-legged.

'After our bath, we have biscuits and blackcurrant juice, and when we go to bed we have a story read.'

'Don't like juice, I want cola,' Liam said stretching out his chubby legs.

'You can't. Mum said it gives you nightmares.'

'Come on, you two, and show me where the bathroom is.'

In the steamy bathroom, Kate bathed first Liam, while Holly, who knew where everything was, brought clean pyjamas. Both children, their faces shining, then sat on the rug drinking juice and munching flapjacks and deciding which story Kate was going to read to them. Diplomatically, Kate read them one each. Liam was asleep long before his story was finished. When Kate tucked both children in, Holly clasped her slender arms about Kate's neck and hugged her, saying, 'I like you.'

A delicious feeling of warmth flooded Kate, as she tenderly stroked Holly's hair.

'And I like you. Friends?'

She held out her little finger and Holly curled hers round Kate's.

' 'Night, 'night,' Kate whispered.

The nightlight cast a gentle glow around the room and the two sleeping children represented to Kate a vision of a make-believe world she could never hope to encounter.

Downstairs she tidied away and washed up. Poor Denise, what a shock to have her mother taken ill and rushed into hospital. She could make some supper but she didn't like to pry into Denise's cupboards so she settled for a mug of coffee and one of the children's flapjacks.

She settled in a comfy chair and picked up a magazine from a pile on the small table. Idly she flicked through it, sipping her coffee, listening to the rhythmic swaying of trees outside. She closed her eyes and the next thing she remembered was hearing Denise's voice.

'I'm sorry I've been so long.'

Yawning, Kate shook herself.

'How's your mother?'

'Comfortable. She's getting medication for a deep vein thrombosis. Poor Mum, she's scared and Dad panicked. He doesn't drive anymore so it will be up to me to take him to hospital and to keep an eye on him so I want to ask you a special favour.'

She paused for breath, sinking wearily into the chair opposite Kate.

'Can I ask you to pick up the children from school for me? Frank can take them in the mornings. It's just until I see how Mum progresses over the next few days.'

'No problem, of course I will. Shall I

make you coffee?'

'I'd rather have wine. Sorry about the meal. I'd made a lasagne earlier and left it in the microwave. Do you want it now?'

'No. Save it for your meal tomorrow.'

Kate was pleased to see the worried look leave Denise's face, and she stayed with her until her husband came home.

Back in Kenjarra House, in her bed, Kate thought about Liam and Holly and how much she had enjoyed being with them. Children are a joy, Kate mused, not a burden as her mother had always said. That night Kate slept soundly and awoke at first light.

Humming a catchy tune, she dressed in jeans and sweatshirt. They were fast becoming her uniform and she loved the casual attire!

Downstairs, she slipped on a pair of wellingtons and grabbed a well-worn jacket off the peg by the side door. Today, instead of making for the mere, she strode in the opposite direction where she hoped to find the gardens

Denise had mentioned. The sun was bright but there was a slight chill in the air. She pulled up the coat collar and dug her hands deep in the coat pockets.

Her heart gave an unexpected lurch as her fingers closed on a crumpled piece of paper. Stopping, she pulled the paper from the pocket and smoothed it out. It was an old envelope with a list of plant names in faded pencil though she couldn't quite make out the scribbling beneath. She held it up to catch more light and read, *Kathryn's Garden*. Slowly she turned the envelope over to see the address — Mr Christopher Mansell, Kenjarra House. Then she turned it back over to gaze at her father's writing. She was born Kathryn Mary Mansell!

Shivering, she leaned against the old brick wall for support, hugging the coat closer. Burying her face into it, she caught a whiff of stale tobacco, fragrance of the garden, and the smell of her father, his coat, and his nearness.

4

'Are you all right?' the voice came, but for a moment Kate forgot where she was and on raising her face, stared stupidly at Nick Duvivier.

He stepped nearer, his touch gentle on her arm.

'Are you ill?'

Thrown by his concern she blurted out, 'It's my father's coat. His list.'

He took the envelope from her trembling outstretched hand and glancing at it, he explained.

'Christopher finished this garden not long before he died. Would you like to see it?'

She nodded. Still feeling shaken, she allowed him to take her arm. She leaned into him for support, her legs moving like a puppet. He led her along a narrow path, one side overhung with trees and bushes and on the other side a high red brick wall. Halfway down, he stopped before a sturdy wooden door set into the wall. Removing a loose brick he withdrew a large black key and unlocked the door, throwing it open.

She followed him through, gasping in amazement as they walked along the mosaic-effect path of different-coloured pebbles edged with a brick border flanked by arches of fragrant white roses climbing up and over a timber pergola.

Reaching the end of the vista, Kate whispered, 'It's so beautiful, magical.'

Not wanting to break the spell, she gazed in wonderment around the walled garden. Centre stage, its focal point, stood a sundial carved in York stone encircled by a pattern of old red bricks edged by neat, clipped box hedging with four paths of lush green grass radiating out.

'This was the old, walled garden of the house, neglected till about five years ago. This is Christopher's life's work and I had the privilege of helping him.

Christopher created the design based on a rug pattern hanging on his study wall.'

She nodded, recalling seeing it, as Nick continued.

'It's a series of garden rooms leading from the centre with each garden leading through to the next. That's the theory when the fifth one is complete.'

She glanced at Nick thinking he was going to say something else, but his eyes were glazed and he seemed to forget she was there. Not moving, she looked around noticing the virgin soil of the plot to be the last garden. She wasn't a gardener, only planting a couple of hanging baskets and tubs, but she could see the vast amount of work required finishing the project. Nick interrupted her thoughts.

'This is why I'm opposed to you selling Kenjarra. I want to see Christopher's dream fulfilled, and for it to be a memorial to him.'

Kate turned sharply to look into his serious face.

'You were very close to my father, weren't you?'

'Yes, I was. I lecture at the local agricultural college and Christopher came along to one of our open days on horticulture. We talked about his idea to renovate the walled garden. He invited me down and whenever I had free time I came to help him. It was a great healer for me, it took my mind off things. Then I rented the old stable block when . . . it was convenient.'

She wanted to ask what he wanted to take his mind off. She didn't, but she wondered.

He started to walk down one of the grass paths towards one of the gardens enclosed by a willow fence, calling over his shoulder, 'This way to Kathryn's Garden.'

She followed him, until he stopped abruptly and she cannoned into him, her face rubbing against the soft wool of his jumper. She inhaled his fresh scent of soap. Her heart gave one of those funny lurches it seemed to perform of late. He half-turned, his brown eyes looking deep into hers.

'Christopher told me that this garden was for a very special person, Kathryn. Is Kate short for Kathryn?' he asked.

'Yes,' she whispered, then to her embarrassment she blushed.

His eyes lingered on her for a moment longer then he turned, continuing along the path. If she thought the first garden was beautiful, Kathryn's Garden surpassed her wildest imagination, a dream, an oasis of tranquillity bathed in every shade of pink imaginable. A drift of phlox filled a corner in varying shades from delicate hint of pink to deep fuchsia, interplanted with shrubs of shining green leaves and variegated foliage.

Turning, she marvelled at the fragrant roses tumbling along the wall, intertwined with clematis. As she walked along a cobbled, winding path, flowers and grasses swayed gently. At the end of the path she caught her breath. On the south-facing wall was an arbour constructed of fretwork trellis laced with honeysuckle, with a bench to sit and meditate or just dream.

She sat down, her eyes filling with tears. Her father must have loved her so much and now she would never have the chance to return his love. He had remembered her favourite colour as a young girl. She brushed away her tears and closed her eyes, seeing his face, smiling.

'Pink to make the boys wink,' he would say to her.

Nick, coming towards her, stopped, and seeing her visibly moved by Christopher's creation she went up in his estimation. It brought a lump to his throat. On first meeting her, he thought her spoiled, money-grabbing, with no feelings for the countryside or Kenjarra House. Now he was beginning to warm to her, but what if she went ahead and sold Kenjarra and the land? Somehow he must persuade her not to sell because his greatest desire was to see Christopher's work here completed.

'Kate.'

She opened her eyes to see Nick watching her. She sat up straight, aware of a strange look in his eyes. Then he glanced at his watch.

'Breakfast time. Maisie will have the bacon sizzling.'

He held out his hand and she took it.

As they entered the kitchen at Kenjarra House, Maisie turned from the stove, glanced at Nick then gave Kate a funny look, but didn't speak. Kate, in a happy mood, didn't wish to interpret what Maisie was thinking. Wilf came in joined by Harry Leland and all of them sat round the kitchen table while the conversation turned to freedom! Harry began to reminisce about his working days.

'Freedom, that's what I had. Freedom to roam any part of the estate. I love the woodlands, the fox and deer, the mere, the gulls,' he rambled.

Kate only half listened until he said, 'I was in the Dog and Duck last night and Bertie Marshall told me the boat club has drawn up plans for when they take over Kenjarra.'

His knife poised in the air he stared accusingly at Kate.

'This is your doing.'

Four pairs of eyes fixed on Kate. She went cold then hot and bit her lip. She was just about to say that she hadn't as yet put Kenjarra on the market when Nick jumped to his feet, his chair scraping the floor.

'You didn't even have the common courtesy to tell us that you have put Kenjarra up for sale,' he said harshly and stormed from the kitchen.

She stared after him. Lowering her eyes and with as much dignity as she could muster, she rose from the table.

'Excuse me,' she muttered.

Angry, she was determined to put Nick Duvivier right. It was all right for him to pontificate but he didn't have the responsibility of making decisions about Kenjarra estate. How did he know what was right? He only thought he did. Hurrying to the stable block, she was just in time to see him hurling down the lane in his Land-Rover. She shouted after him, but of course he didn't hear her. Deflated, she turned and slowly walked back to the house. To avoid the others in the kitchen she entered by the front door and went upstairs.

In a daze, she found herself in her father's room. Going over to the bureau she sat down, resting her throbbing head against the cool, polished oak. Minutes ticked on the wall clock and she wished her life could be suspended in time, but a voice in her head said that was a coward's way out. Sighing deeply, Kate knew she must face up to her responsibilities.

Swiftly, she rose to her feet and went back along the corridor to her own room. Pulling her mobile phone and address book from her handbag, flicking through the pages until she found her late father's solicitor's telephone number, she punched it out.

'Hello, this is Mrs Kathryn Byron

here. I wish to make an appointment with Mr Carrick.'

'Certainly, madam,' the efficient secretary replied. 'May I ask the nature of your business?'

'It's regarding my late father's estate, Kenjarra House.'

'Ah, yes, Mrs Byron, Mr Carrick has been waiting for you to be in touch. Two o'clock tomorrow afternoon, would that be convenient?'

'Yes.'

Kate stood staring out of the window towards the mere. The sunlight played on the water like tiny fairies in golden dresses dancing in sequence. She would miss this beautiful view. Abruptly she turned and left the room, making her way back to her father's room. Realising she still had her mobile in her hand, she decided to ring Aunt Rosemary. She needed to hear a friendly voice.

'Hello, dear. Lovely to hear from you,' Rosemary's warm voice tinkled across the miles, bringing her close.

Kate felt a lump in her throat and a

sudden idea jumped into her mind. This very weekend she would drive down to see Aunt Rosemary.

'I have some wonderful news,' Rosemary said.

'What is it, Aunt?'

'Remember Jean Blaketon I was at school with?'

Kate laughed.

'I don't remember her because I wasn't born then, but I know who you mean.'

'Well, she has asked me to go on holiday to Indonesia with her. She has a son who lives and works just outside of Jakarta and he and his wife are going to take us on a grand tour. Isn't that marvellous? I'm so thrilled and I've so much to do before I go.'

'That's wonderful for you, Aunt. Is there anything I can do? I can come down this weekend.'

'That's kind of you, dear, but you have enough to do. I can manage. But before I go I'll go and see Joshua.'

'Joshua?'

Then it came to her who he was — Vincent's son. She had forgotten about him! She let her aunt chatter on then Rosemary said, 'I must dash now, dear. I've an appointment with the hairdresser.'

Instead of feeling uplifted, Kate once again felt down. Of course, she was pleased for her aunt, but it seemed that everyone she loved or cared for was slipping away from her. Waves of loneliness engulfed her, weakening her resolve to stay to wind up her father's affairs. The temptation to pack her suitcase, climb into her car and turn her back on Kenjarra was strong. But she had promised Denise to collect Liam and Holly from school that afternoon.

She sat at the bureau, and unlocking it she began her task. As she was going to see the solicitor tomorrow she needed to be aware if her father had left her any instructions, though what, she couldn't imagine, but like Kathryn's Garden there might be something.

She opened a small, leather-bound

book. It was a journal of jottings of Christopher Mansell. He was born between the two wars, living near Derby; he came north to Driffield to do his National Service in the RAF.

A few pages on she read, *I was at the monthly social camp when I met Dorinda, a fascinating creature who flirted outrageously with me. When I asked her for a date she insisted that her friend, Violet, came along. Violet was a quiet girl with lovely blue eyes and a warm smile*.

'Dorinda,' Kate said aloud. 'Now where have I heard the name before?'

She pondered then recalled Harry telling her that Dorinda had drowned in the mere. Dorinda and her mother had been friends and yet she had never heard her mother mention the name. Quite odd, too, as she had never suspected her mother of having a warm smile. Kate wondered what had happened to change her mother so.

A knock came at the door and it opened to reveal Maisie.

'I've brought you a coffee,' she said then her eyes fell on the array of papers and the journal in Kate's hand.

'Sorry to disturb you.'

'Come in. The coffee's welcome. Maisie, did you know a woman called Dorinda Whitely?'

'There used to be a family called Whitely, but they moved on before we came here.'

She placed the mug of coffee on a place mat on top of bureau, then made towards the door.

'Are you coming down for lunch?' she asked.

'No, but I'd be grateful if you brought me up a sandwich and an apple.'

She turned back to the journal but it seemed only to cover estate matters, then as she flicked through the pages, a folded piece of paper fell out. She smoothed it out.

It was torn from an exercise book as if in a hurry and written in pencil was a short message: *I must see you as soon as possible. I will be down by the mere at eight. D.*

Kate drew in her breath sharply when she saw what was written on the journal page.

Violet went out and Kathryn was fretful so I could not leave her to go and meet D.

If her father had married Violet, why would he be having a clandestine meeting with D, and was it Dorinda? Kate rubbed her eyes. The journal intrigued her but she must press on to other matters.

Looking through sheaves of paper she came across a manila folder containing some official correspondence from a firm of chartered accountants in London, concerning inheritance tax. She read through the documents, not too sure if she fully understood, but she would take it with her to the solicitor's. A quick glance at her wristwatch told her she had over an hour before she collected the children from school, time for a freshening shower.

She arrived early in Burtonsea. Parking in the supermarket carpark, she wandered down the High Street, mingling with the summer visitors. She window-shopped and, coming to an estate agent on the corner near to the school, she was tempted to go inside, but she didn't want to be late for the children. So she contented herself with the window display, surprised how low house prices were in this area.

Unknown to her, Nick Duvivier was driving down the High Street. He stopped at the zebra crossing near the school to let a couple cross when he saw Kate looking in the estate agent's window. Oh, no, he thought! She really means to sell Kenjarra. He watched to see if she was going inside but a horn sounded behind him and he had to move. When he glanced in his rear view mirror she had gone. He felt like a spear had pierced his body.

5

Returning Holly and Liam home to Lilac Cottage from school, Kate offered to look after the children while Denise and her husband, Frank, went to visit her mother in hospital.

'Are you sure?' Denise asked, looking strained.

'Of course. You be off and don't worry. The children will be fine with me.'

She watched them go, feeling a little guilty. This cottage was a bolthole for her at the moment. She couldn't face a meal at Kenjarra House, not after the episode at breakfast, nor did she want the alternative of eating alone in the dining-room.

Once she had seen the solicitor she might be in a better position to inform Maisie, Wilf, Harry and Nick what was going to happen.

'Kate, I'm hungry,' Liam said, tugging at her arm.

She slipped her hand into his hot little fist and it felt comforting.

'Come on, let me see what I can find.'

'Noodles?' he said hopefully.

'I can help,' Holly said, taking hold of Kate's other hand.

Kate's heart filled with a special feeling, a wonderful experience she wished she could keep for ever.

Her voice strangely hoarse, she replied, 'That's lovely. You can show me where everything is.'

It was nearly midnight when Kate left Lilac Cottage. Denise and Frank had brought home a Chinese takeaway and they had thoroughly enjoyed the meal. Denise's mother was much better and responding to medication and the younger daughter was coming to stay with her father to help lessen the burden. Kate declined Frank's offer to walk her home. It was such a lovely night, a bright, starlit sky with a half-moon sending shafts of silver beams through the branches of overhead trees.

She breathed in the soft air, catching the smell of apple logs burning somewhere. Her step was jaunty and she hummed a catchy tune. For the time being her problems were forgotten. She felt happy and carefree. Maybe it was the combination of food, wine, good company and the children, but whatever, it was a great tonic.

Passing the walled garden, a lighthearted idea struck her. What fun it would be to have the gardens aglow with night-lights, nothing garish. Now she was becoming fanciful. A sudden movement ahead made her stop and she glanced about, seeing nothing. She strained her eyes as the moon disappeared behind a cloud and the garden wall cast shadows.

Her heart thudded.

Don't be silly she told herself. You're in the countryside and nocturnal creatures prowl at night. Her steps quickened towards the house, her breathing rapid, when suddenly she felt the rough hair of an animal brush against her legs. She screamed, every muscle in her body tightening. A dog barked.

Somewhere an owl hooted and amidst this night cacophony a man's stern voice called, 'Heel, Bramble.'

In the flash of his torchlight, Kate saw the grim face of Nick Duvivier and her heart sank. He was the last person she wanted to see. Her legs shaky, she staggered forward but with her head held high was intent on passing him without speaking. But he blocked her way.

He didn't move but said, 'Did you have to bring the cheap, low life of the city here?'

Shocked by his words and realising he thought her the worst for drink she retaliated.

'Mr Duvivier, I do not have to explain myself to you. Please step aside and let me pass.'

He did, yet she was conscious of his eyes following her till she reached the front door. Once inside the house, she hurried up the stairs to her room and flung off her clothes.

'Damn that man,' she muttered as she got ready for bed.

The next morning, Kate awoke around seven feeling rather groggy. She stumbled from her bed to the bathroom to have a good, long soak. Refreshed, her skin sparkling, she dressed and went down to the kitchen to make herself coffee and toast. She wanted to disappear before anyone else came in for breakfast, but Maisie had beaten her to it. They exchanged greetings and Kate poured a mug of coffee from the pot on the stove and buttered a round of toast.

'I've a lot to do this morning, so I best get on,' she said, hurrying from the kitchen before Maisie could utter a word.

Carrying her mug of coffee and munching toast, she went up to her father's room. She crossed the carpeted floor to the main window but she couldn't open it. It had jammed. The smaller window on the narrower side wall opened with little effort. Leaning out over the sill she could see the stable block yard and Nick Duvivier.

He whistled to Bramble as they began their morning walk. Watching him, she was conscious of his tall, powerful body moving with ease and confidence. He ran a hand through his dark hair leaving it tousled. As he drew nearer to the house, he suddenly glanced up and their eyes locked for a few seconds. He raised his hand in a half-mocking salute. Ignoring it she quickly stepped back out of his view, experiencing a queer sensation in her stomach, as if it was performing a double somersault.

Making an effort, she settled down, and dismissing Nick Duvivier from her mind, she picked up the folder marked Inheritance Tax. She needed to see if she could make more sense of it before going to see the solicitor.

Later that afternoon, Thomas Carrick, solicitor of Marshall, Marshall & Carrick watched from his first-floor office window in Market Place as Kate Byron alighted from her car. She was smartly dressed in a navy trouser suit and cream top and carrying a briefcase. He snorted to himself. City girls! What do they know? And city men for that matter.

Christopher Mansell had never heeded his advice. Instead he preferred playing the country squire. That was the only reason Violet had married Mansell and not himself. She saw herself as the lady bountiful but then Dorinda put a spoke in the wheel.

Still, he had been sorry when Violet fled. She should have come to him. He would have taken care of her, loved her. Now he was content to see the disintegration of Mansell's little empire. He puffed out his broad chest. As president of the boat club, his ability to acquire full access to Kenjarra Mere would ensure that he had a prestigious position in the club's history.

Kate had a positive feeling as she sat down opposite Mr Carrick.

'I was expecting you to contact me earlier, Mrs Byron. I understand you wish to sell Kenjarra House and the adjoining land and I have prepared the necessary documents for you to sign.'

He smiled, not so much at her but at his achievement.

Kate's positive feeling remained as she answered him coolly.

'You have obviously been misinformed, Mr Carrick. I have no intentions of selling Kenjarra or the land. I think that would not be in keeping with my late father's wish.'

His florid face went even redder and he shuffled his feet.

'Mrs Byron, financially you have no option but to sell.'

'I think you are wrong. My father was a very wise man. He made adequate provisions for Kenjarra.'

From her briefcase she withdrew the folder marked Inheritance Tax and handed it to Mr Carrick.

'I think you will find this will explain everything,' she said sweetly.

* * *

Now that the decision not to sell Kenjarra was made, Kate needed to talk to someone about it, someone objective, like Denise. She drew up outside Lilac Cottage, relieved to find Denise at home.

As she stepped into the homely kitchen she said, 'I didn't know if you would be at the hospital.'

'Dad's going. I want to meet the kids from school. I've neglected them over the last couple of days. I'll pop in and see Mum later when they're in bed. Tea, coffee?'

'Tea, please.'

Kate sat down at the kitchen table and before she could think, everything that had happened at the solicitor's office came pouring out. Denise listened, not interrupting until Kate had finished talking.

Then she said, 'How are you going to make up for the shortfall of money?'

'I'm not sure, but I won't be beaten. As Aunt Rosemary would say, put on your thinking cap.'

Back in Kenjarra House, Kate found Maisie polishing silver in the dining-room.

'Can you ask Harry and Nick to come for dinner tonight? I've something important I want to discuss.'

Maisie didn't offer any comment, just nodded unsmilingly and as soon as Kate went she threw down her polishing cloth and went in search of Wilf.

Tears in her eyes, Maisie found Wilf in the yard at the back of the house stocking up on logs for the winter.

'A waste of time you doing that. We won't be here to enjoy the log fires.'

Wilf glanced up, rubbing the sweat from his weather-beaten face.

'What do you mean?'

He straightened up and leaned against the wall of the fuel store.

'She's going to tell us all tonight that she's selling up. She's just come back from the solicitor's. We can say goodbye to our cottage by the sea.'

And with that the tears came cascading down her cheeks. Big, burly Wilf, not usually demonstrative, took his sobbing wife into his arms.

'Don't take on so, lass. Something will turn up.'

When told what Maisie thought was happening Harry said, 'Well, I can tell yer, no bloomin' boat official is gonna keep me from walking those woods.'

Nick was quieter.

'So it's come then, though I thought there might have been a chance she wouldn't sell.'

He was remembering the morning he had shown her Kathryn's Garden. He must have imagined her spark of enthusiasm.

That evening, when Kate entered the

kitchen, it was to find four subdued faces at the kitchen table.

'Good evening,' she said cheerfully.

One of them grunted in reply but she wasn't sure who it was. Maisie placed a huge casserole dish on the table and lifted off the lid and instantly the kitchen was full of the rich aroma of duck. She proceeded to serve, handing round the plates and all the time no-one spoke. Kate tried to think of how to start the conversation, but it was as if there was an invisible shield blocking them from speaking.

She manoeuvred her food around her plate, her appetite gone. Suddenly something within her snapped and she jumped to her feet, her chair grating on the floor as she shoved it back. Like puppets on a string, all four of them looked up and stared at her.

'I'm not selling Kenjarra!' she blurted out.

She felt close to tears, but they were tears of frustration. There was total silence. Her facial muscles tightened.

Then Harry said, 'By, that's one in the eye for the toffee-nose boat club. They thought they had it made.'

Kate felt her tension lessening, but she remained standing. She looked round the table waiting for someone else to speak. It was Nick.

'So this is it! It's all a game to you. You've put us through agony and now you want us to be grateful.'

His anger was obvious. She stared at him in disbelief. Whatever response she had expected from him it certainly wasn't this. Then without another word, he rose from the table and left the kitchen. The clock above the dresser ticked loudly. Harry glanced at it.

'Time I was off to the pub. I promised to make up a domino foursome.'

Wilf mumbled something about a blocked drain and he went so it only left Maisie and Kate. Kate slumped down on her chair, resting her elbows on the table. She buried her face in her hands then she heard the tap of

Maisie's shoes as she also left the kitchen. Alone, all she could think was that she had made a ghastly mistake. Her instinct must be wrong but now she had committed herself to the preservation of Kenjarra and with or without their help she would do it.

A light touch on her shoulder made her jump and she lifted up her head to look into Maisie's concerned face.

'Drink this, lass, a tot of brandy. Do you good.'

Kate clasped the goblet in both hands and sipped the golden liquid, letting it seep into her numbed body. Maisie sat down opposite and she didn't speak until Kate had drained the glass.

'Don't take to heart what Nick said. It came as a shock to us all. We were expecting you to say that you were selling up and our thoughts were on those lines. Nick loves Kenjarra, more than Wilf and me.'

Kate looked across at the older woman, not able to forgive Nick for such cruel words so personally directed at her.

'He thinks I was gloating but that isn't my style. Now the decision is made to keep Kenjarra, I wanted to discuss with you all how we could raise enough money to keep on running it.'

'That is a problem, lass, and one you shouldn't carry alone. I'll have a word with the three men, and tomorrow night we will sit down to dinner and we'll have no arguing. I shall warn them, have no fear.'

Kate smiled, glad of Maisie's support, but she doubted if Nick Duvivier would give her his full support. How could he when he obviously hated her so much?

6

The next day Kate kept herself busy. She had slipped a small notepad and pencil into the pocket of her jeans to jot down any ideas that came flowing for raising money for the upkeep of Kenjarra. Mid-morning, she found herself taking a rest on the bench in the sweet-scented arbour of Kathryn's Garden and with the sun warm on her face, the fragrance of rose and honeysuckle filling her nostrils, she closed her eyes.

It was so peaceful here, listening to the drone of the bees, the singing of a distant blackbird and the rhythmic gurgle of water tinkling from the tiny pebble water feature. The notepad lying idle on her lap fell unheeded on to the cobblestones at her feet and she drifted off into a calming lull.

The sun disappearing behind a cloud

woke her with a cool shudder. She yawned and stretched, sighing. She had been dreaming of designing a magnificent garden for the Chelsea Flower Show! She retrieved her notepad and glanced at her comments, which were trivial in comparison and were nothing that made any financial sense.

In its private library, Kenjarra had hundreds of books and she would just need to catalogue them, then turn Kenjarra into a hotel, but would she want to share her home with strangers?

From the balmy air around her, ideas began to tumble into her mind . . . open the gardens and grounds to visitors . . . let people see the beautiful Kenjarra Mere in a natural woodland setting . . . nature trails for school children. Would Harry be willing to help? And maybe Maisie would fancy making cream teas. Nick? She would have to build bridges with him. If her plans were to succeed she needed Nick's help. His expertise in horticulture would be of invaluable help to her together with his manpower.

That evening, filled with renewed vigour, Kate discarded her jeans and T-shirt and surveyed her limited wardrobe. Most of her clothes were still at Aunt Rosemary's. The trouser suit she had worn to the solicitor's was too formal, even though this was to be a working dinner. Finally she settled on a pair of slim-fitting trousers, a satin camisole in burgundy and a matching overshirt with satin collar and cuffs. Her newly-washed hair shone like silk and she left it loose.

Sitting at her dressing-table, she applied only the minimum of make-up finishing off with lip-gloss. Then selecting a pair of black kitten-heeled shoes she was ready, ready to do battle if necessary, though a little nervous. Armed with her neatly-arranged notes she went downstairs.

She found the kitchen empty and not set for dinner, but pans were bubbling on the hob and that was reassuring. Searching for Maisie, she found her in the dining-room and was surprised to see her putting the finishing touches to the table there.

Kate stood on the threshold viewing the room. Although it was late summer and not particularly cold, a log fire smelling of apple wood burned brightly in the grate. It gave out a mellow glow reflecting on the faded wall decorations and on the polished sideboard, adding welcoming warmth to the room that in the past she had only thought of as cold and uninviting. She took a step forward.

Maisie glanced up and gave a huge smile, saying, 'I've told them to dress smartly and to be on their best behaviour or I'll go on strike and won't cook for them.'

Kate laughed, relaxing her feeling of tension. She didn't see Nick come into the room and stare at her.

'Good evening,' he said softly.

Turning she faced him.

'Good evening.'

They didn't notice Maisie quietly

leave the room. His face was serious, but Kate, looking deep into his eyes, thought she detected a hint of, what? Averting her eyes she made pretence of straightening out an invisible crease in the damask tablecloth.

'Kate.'

'Yes?' she answered, not looking up.

'I'm sorry. I was out of order last night. I shouldn't have spoken to you as I did.'

He came closer to her and her heart began its now familiar intimate routine of somersaulting whenever Nick was close to her.

'Friends?' he said and held out his hand.

She took it, feeling his strength.

'I'd rather have you as a friend than an enemy.'

Now he laughed, his tanned skin crinkling around his sparkling eyes.

'Consider it done.'

On an impulse, he leaned forward and kissed her on the cheek. To hide her confusion, she also laughed. Then from the cooler on the table, Nick lifted a bottle of white wine and poured two glasses, giving one to Kate.

'Here's to friendship.'

Their raised glasses touched and to Kate it felt as if they were the only two people in the world.

'Any beer?'

Harry came trundling into the room, breaking the spell, and soon Wilf and Maisie joined them. Kate glanced round the table once they were seated and the atmosphere was light as they all began to chat amicably. She gave a sigh of pure contentment. Nick looked across the table at her and winked, and she winked back at him!

Ideas were soon being thrashed about. Harry liked the idea of being a guide for the woodland walk for groups of school children.

'I could give 'em nature quizzes and treasure hunts.'

'Harry, are you sure it won't be too much for you?' Kate asked.

'Nay, lass. I was just thinking.

There're a few fallen trees around and they could be placed in clearings for when I tell children stories. I've a couple of strapping lads in mind to help me.'

Maisie offered to serve any refreshments necessary and keep the house in good order, with the help of Wilf who would man the gate and fetch and carry where needed.

'I'll make a start on repairing fences,' he said obligingly.

Kate looked to Nick.

'That leaves the garden. What do you think?'

Sipping his wine and leaning back in his chair, Nick said, 'First you need to finish the last garden. Christopher had plans to create a Victorian conservatory. Perhaps with fewer plants in it, we could have indoor seating for visitors in case it rains.'

Kate smiled.

'I like that. I want to follow my father's design as much as possible. How long will it take?'

Nick considered for a moment.

'If I can persuade some of my students to volunteer their services, we could be up and running by spring, but for the building of the Victorian conservatory, I would advise getting in professionals.'

Maisie came in with a steaming pot of coffee and set it down on the table and began to pour, joining in the conversation.

'Why not ask Denise to suggest to her aerobics class about having an exercise day planting bulbs along the woodland trail? All that bending will be good for the figure,' she suggested, adding with a mischievous grin, 'I can give them tea and cakes to replace the calories.'

'Maisie, you are an angel,' Kate said, accepting a cup of coffee.

After the coffee Nick looked across at Kate.

'Fancy a walk to the gardens? There's enough light left for us to have a look around.'

'Sure. Just give me a second to change into sensible shoes.'

A few minutes later, they strolled companionably side by side. The decision Kate had made to stay at Kenjarra and see her father's project through filled her with a wonderful sense of the unknown, of an adventure and of hard work, and of the latter she had no illusions. But what made it exciting was she would be working with Nick. Now they both desired the same goal, hopefully there wouldn't be any animosity between them.

She must ring Aunt Rosemary to tell her the news. She would be surprised, or would she? In a couple of weeks her aunt would be off on her travels. Kate would miss her, but the project would keep her busy.

'Penny for them?'

Nick broke into her thoughts. She laughed and found herself telling him about her aunt.

'She's not a real aunt, a distant cousin of my mother's, but she's my godmother and I love her dearly. You'll get to meet her one day.'

'I'll look forward to that.'

He opened the door to the walled garden and took hold of her elbow, guiding her through. The touch of his hand sent quivers of pleasure through her. How could a man whom she didn't really know inject such feelings into her like this?

She was content just to be with Nick and he was obviously happy to be with her. They strolled around the main garden and the three smaller gardens until they came to the bare plot. Kate stared at the bare soil trying to imagine how it would look when the garden was completed. But she couldn't.

'Where is my father's plan for this garden?'

Nick, close by her side replied, 'I have it.'

'Perhaps I should see it. I need to see and feel what my father wanted.'

'Your wish is my command, fair lady.'

Kate laughed a low, sensual sound

and Nick had a sudden desire to take her into his arms, but he held back and the moment was lost as Kate moved off. They approached the disused stables where Nick had a small apartment above. He started to mount the wooden stairs.

'I'm sorry, I'm intruding. I didn't realise the plans were in your private quarters,' Kate said.

Nick looked over his shoulder, grinning at her.

'No problem. Come on up.'

She followed him up into his sitting-room. One wall was lined with bookshelves full to capacity and the opposite wall was taken up with a brick fireplace with exposed beams and an enclosed wood-burning stove with a pile of logs nearby. Covering the polished, wooden floor was a rug in blending shades of red and sitting on it was a comfortable-looking sofa full of scatter cushions of various patterns.

By the fireplace were an armchair and a book lying open on top of a small table. Kate couldn't resist peeping at the title, **John Halifax, Gentleman**. She remembered reading that book in her youth. The room had a welcoming, relaxing feel to it. They say a home reflects its inhabitant and Kate smiled to herself, wondering.

'Take a seat. I'll get the plans. But first would you like a nightcap?' Nick offered.

'Please. Whisky with dry will be fine.'

It was a long time since she had had a nightcap with a man. When she and Vincent were first married they did indulge, until her miscarriage. Nick witnessed the shadow of sadness that passed across Kate's face.

'Are you all right?' he asked, concerned.

'Fine,' she replied automatically.

He'd seen that look on her face before. Obviously she must still be grieving for her husband who, he understood, died in a road accident. She never talked about him and he didn't like to mention the subject. Time is a healer, so it is said and, yes, he supposed he could testify to that experience.

He handed Kate her glass and sat beside her on the sofa.

'Here's to the future of Kenjarra and to all of us involved.'

They raised their glasses.

They talked long into the night, mostly mulling over Christopher's plan for the final garden, seeing which plants could be omitted from the conservatory without spoiling the overall effect. Kate could feel the heaviness of her eyelids and fought to keep them open, never wanting this magical evening to end. She couldn't remember when she had last felt so happy.

'Time I was taking you back to the house,' Nick broke into her ramblings.

'There's no need for you to come out again,' she began but he cut her short.

'I want to, and Bramble needs his walk.'

The night was dark and Nick placed

a casual arm about Kate's shoulder, welcoming the feel of her warmth close to him. It had been a long time since he had felt a tender passion towards a woman. His ex-wife had taken care of that along with his confidence and trust.

Despite their shaky start, he instinctively felt he could trust Kate even though he had been prepared to fight her on the issue of Kenjarra. He wouldn't rush things, not declare his feelings for her just yet, but give her time and space while she grieved for her dead husband.

As she stepped out along the darkened path Kate caught her foot on the protruding root of a tree, stumbling into Nick. His arm tightened around her and they were suddenly locked in an embrace, face to face, with only one thing to do and there was no holding back.

The sensation of warm lips touching hers sent shivers of pure delight through Kate's body. Then suddenly

Nick drew away from her, leaving her startled.

'Sorry,' he muttered.

Puzzled, she looked at his face, so pale in the darkness.

Softly she said, 'Don't be. I wasn't.'

He didn't answer and they walked in silence to the house. On reaching the door and with the aid of the porch light Kate searched Nick's eyes, but it was as if a shutter had been pulled down.

'Thank you for an interesting, informative evening,' she said, then on impulse she stood on tiptoe and kissed his cheek and whispered, 'I've loved every minute.'

He stared at her, unable to speak.

Her courage deserting her, she fled indoors.

Slowly, Nick walked round the house until he saw a lone light in one of the bedrooms that he knew must be Kate's. He leaned against a tree trunk while Bramble sniffed around.

That girl had found in him his most vulnerable spot, the need to love and be loved. He thought he could handle it, but her warmth had come so unexpectedly and he had frozen. Had he blown it?

Whistling for Bramble, he turned from the house, not seeing the figure at the window peering out.

Kate stood at the window staring out at the darkness. She had willed Nick to kiss her again but he hadn't, and now she was having illusions imagining she could see him outside looking wistfully up at her bedroom window. She drew the curtains. She was angry with herself for letting her emotions surface so readily. After all, Nick had only promised to help to get the gardens up and running, nothing else.

Then why did he kiss her with such warmth and passion? Perhaps that was just his way and she had read too much into it. Was she so vulnerable? The shock of Vincent's untimely death must have hit her harder than she supposed and she was grabbing at any man who showed her a molecule of affection. She must try to concentrate on the practicalities of life, like work and more work, and try to ignore the terrible feeling of loneliness that often crept up on her like an unwelcome visitor.

As she burrowed under the comfort of the duvet, she wondered if her heart would remain forever unfulfilled.

Next morning she was up bright and early with clipboard in hand, mobile phone and the Yellow Pages, and began the quotation quest for the conservatory. She made appointments for various representatives to call. Things were moving and she felt pleased with her morning's work.

For the rest of the week she was quite busy, with no time to fill her head with foolish romantic nonsense. But before the onslaught of work commenced in earnest, she took a walk down to Lilac Cottage to see Denise and to enquire after her mother's health.

'Come in, lovely to see you,' Denise welcomed on opening the door to Kate.

'You don't mind the kitchen? I'm on a mammoth bake.'

Kate followed her friend into the kitchen where a delicious aroma greeted her. She glanced at the centre table and the work surfaces, all full of cakes and savoury pastries cooling on wire trays.

'You are busy and I'm interrupting you.'

'No, last batch is in and I'm due for a well-earned break. Tea or coffee?'

'Coffee's fine. Can I do anything to help?'

'Just sit yourself down. Everything is under control.'

Soon there was a pot of steaming coffee and a plate of hot, buttered scones set on the table space cleared by Denise.

'What brings you here? Anything special?' Denise asked, thinking Kate looked a bit peaky.

'I've come to see how your mother is.'

'She's improving daily and hopefully

she'll be home next week. Now tell me your news.'

Kate launched into the plans for the gardens and grounds and Maisie's suggestion that Denise's aerobics class might like to take part in helping to plant bulbs along the woodland walk. Denise poured more coffee.

'Sounds a great idea. I'll put it to my class, but it can't be this weekend,' she said.

'Of course not. Anytime over the next month or October will do.'

Denise laughed, her warm eyes twinkling.

'Are you free this Saturday by the way?'

Kate looked enquiringly at her friend.

'I've nothing special planned. Do you want me to look after the children?'

'No, this is social. I mentioned to you that my sister is coming over to stay with Dad and help with Mum when she comes out of hospital.'

Kate nodded, vaguely remembering.

'She is coming on Friday night, so I'm arranging a get-together to welcome her and to meet a few people on Saturday, hence all this baking. I'm inviting you to come. You'll like Raquel. She works for a holiday company.'

'I'd love to come. Thanks for inviting me, and I'm sure I'll like your sister.'

On her way back to Kenjarra House, Kate couldn't stop herself wondering if Nick was also invited to the party . . .

For the rest of the week Kate kept busy, avoiding the evening meal when she knew Nick would be there, either by eating earlier or having a snack in her room. By Friday she had seen all the representatives for the conservatory and she decided on a George Collins. He ran a small, family business with his two sons.

George hadn't given her any slick sales patter, not like some of the others and she found his advice strong and his ideas sensible. She felt an instant rapport with him, and he was going to submit his estimate in writing. But she acknowledged it was only common courtesy to inform Nick of her decision.

So that evening Kate made an appearance at dinner and asked Nick if she could speak to him. She kept her voice matter-of-fact but pleasant.

'I'd like to go over the plan for the Victorian conservatory, if you have time.'

'Sure,' he answered but his face was expressionless.

Maisie, bustling about the kitchen, her keen eye aware of tension between the two, interrupted.

'Wilf's lit the fire in the sitting-room. It's more comfortable in there and I'll bring your coffee through.'

Stiffly, Kate followed Nick along the corridor. The sitting-room did indeed look warm and inviting with a cheery fire and soft lamps giving an intimate glow. The rich red velvet curtains were drawn against the night and the chintz-covered sofa beckoned. Kate placed her folder on the low table and promptly sank into the sofa, not looking at Nick who had gone to stand near the fireplace. She felt tired, drained of energy from the challenging pace she had set herself that week.

'Here we are, my lovelies.'

Maisie entered the room carrying a tray laden with a huge pot of coffee, two mugs and two goblets of brandy. Setting the tray down on the low table in front of the sofa she said, 'Thought the brandy might revive those little grey cells after you've both had such a busy week. I'll say goodnight. Wilf and me are going to watch a game show on telly.'

Kate pulled herself up on to the edge of the sofa.

'Goodnight, Maisie, and thanks.'

' 'Night.'

Nick came and sat on the farthest end of the sofa away from Kate.

'Shall I pour?' Kate said, her voice too bright.

'Fine.'

Anger boiled within her. Fine! He

was acting like a sulking child. Why?

'Perhaps you should have your brandy first,' she said and couldn't keep the sarcasm out of her voice.

He replied evenly, 'I think we both need the brandy.'

She glanced at him, seeing the tired lines etched around his eyes and the slight slump of his normally upright body.

'Yes, you're right,' she agreed.

They sipped their brandies, both staring into the magnetic flames of the fire, both wondering what the other was thinking. Except for the occasional crack and sizzle of burning apple logs the room remained silent. Kate broke the stillness.

'Maisie is a very wise person. The brandy has done the trick. I don't feel so tetchy now,' she said, managing a flicker of a smile.

Nick responded with, 'It's been a beastly week for me. First term of the new course year and more than usual unforeseen problems with the new intake of students. Sorry to be such a bore.'

He stared into his empty brandy glass as Kate poured the coffee and passed him a mug.

'We can leave the discussion until a more convenient time, if you wish.'

She was feeling a little guilty because she hadn't considered Nick having any other responsibilities than to Kenjarra. Their fingers touched as he grasped the mug and Kate couldn't stop herself from looking deep into Nick's eyes.

Unexpectedly, she was rewarded with one of his famous twinkles as he in turn looked deep into hers. A lovely warm feeling enveloped her. Maybe it wouldn't be such a bad evening after all.

Nick relaxed back on the sofa, stretching out his long legs.

'This evening is fine for me but let's unwind with our coffee first then you can bring me up to date with the developments.'

He agreed with her choice of contractor.

'George Collins is a fine craftsman. I've seen his work at the college.'

Kate felt pleased and it added to her confidence. They discussed the various plants for the garden, agreeing that the hard landscaping should be kept to the minimal.

Exhilarated, Kate exclaimed, 'I can't wait for work to commence. It's such an exciting project.'

Nick laughed, feeling gratified by her enthusiasm.

'I think we will make a great team if we don't allow our personal differences to interfere with progress.'

She was quick to reply.

'Certainly, but I will respect my own opinions.'

He eyed her quizzically.

'You're tougher than I thought.'

'Yes, I am,' she agreed, her confidence soaring even higher.

Bringing herself down to earth, however, she rose from the sofa and stacked the tray and was just about to whisk it through to the kitchen when Nick intervened, taking it from her.

'Allow me.'

In the kitchen, Nick washed up and she dried. She was just about to say goodnight to him when he said, 'Bramble needs his walk. Do you fancy coming along?'

Her heart gave one of its leaps. How could she refuse him?

'It will be nice to see Bramble.'

She slipped on a pair of wellies and an old jacket and off they went to collect the dog. Bramble was indeed pleased to see her, fussing over her like an old friend.

Animals have good sensitivity, she thought, more than humans do!

As the dog scampered on ahead, Nick said, 'He's a good companion.'

Jokingly, Kate replied, 'He doesn't answer back.'

'I don't get all my own way with him.'

'How long have you been on your own?'

She hadn't meant to say it only think it, but he didn't reply. An owl hooted, perhaps as it swooped to catch a fleeing mouse and Bramble charged in to see what he could do.

'Five years.'

Kate stopped walking, turning to him.

'I am sorry, I didn't mean to pry.'

'It's no secret and it's no longer painful. My wife left me for my best friend. We lived near the college and our house was always open to colleagues and students. Jeff and I worked together and shared most things though I didn't expect to share my wife with him.'

'Is he still at the college?'

'No. They've gone down south. They are no longer of any importance in my life.'

She didn't know what else to say, though his next words took her by surprise.

'What about you?'

Her face drained of colour and she

felt numb. A warm hand touched her arm.

'You don't have to answer. I know you are still grieving. I had no right to ask such a question.'

She leaned into him and his arm went about her waist, supporting her. He guided her to a fallen tree trunk and they sat down. She found her voice, though a bit quaky.

'It's OK. I'm not grieving now. You see, Vincent was killed in a car crash along with his mistress, his secretary. They had been having an affair for four years, ever since I had a miscarriage and was ill for quite a while. He was very understanding.'

Her eyes filled with tears and she couldn't bring herself to tell Nick about Vincent's love child. Perhaps later? Nick didn't speak but held her close and she felt safe. Bramble came back, nuzzling his wet nose against Kate's hand. She drew away from Nick.

'Sorry to unburden myself on you,' she whispered.

He caught her hand.

'Kate, we are friends. Let's be here for each other.'

Her eyes adjusted to the darkness of the night, and she looked into his eyes. Could she see hope? Instinctively she hugged him.

'Thanks,' she whispered.

Bramble barked, no doubt getting bored, and Nick pulled Kate up from the log and slipped his arm through hers.

He murmured into her ear, 'It's been quite a night.'

A wave of unexpected pleasure surged through her body as if a pressure valve had been released.

The next day, Kate worked in the walled garden, entirely alone. She went from garden to garden, tidying up, dead-heading, and marvelling at her late father's creative achievements. The gardens provided a sanctuary of tranquillity and, running her fingers through the soft lushness of the green ferns, Kate felt close to her father.

Sensing his presence all around her she experienced an inner calming of peace. She lost track of time and it was late afternoon before she was kicking off her muddy wellies outside the back door of the house. She followed the smell of food into the kitchen where Maisie was busy pouring boiling water into a brown earthenware teapot.

On seeing Kate she remarked, 'You've timed that nicely. I've made a lemon sponge and fruit loaf.'

Kate, realising she hadn't eaten since breakfast, replied, 'Sounds great.'

She went over to the sink to scrub her hands.

'Are you and Wilf going to the party at Denise's?' she asked.

'No. Wilf's not one for socialising.'

'Come with me, Maisie.'

'No. It wouldn't be right. I'm quite happy just watching telly.'

Kate sat down, helping herself to a generous slice of cake.

'Delicious,' she murmured, and while eating, a thought struck her. 'I've never done any entertaining here,' she said.

'How do you mean?' Maisie asked.

'I'm not sure, but I think there has to be a good reason for it.'

'When Denise's aerobics class comes to plant bulbs, we can have an afternoon tea party. That's an occasion,' Maisie suggested.

'Yes, I suppose you're right.'

But Kate was thinking of something much grander, like filling the house with happy, laughing people, and children?

'Perhaps a party at Christmas?' she said.

'The church choir always comes and sings carols and Mr Mansell provided hot mince pies and punch. A nice tradition,' Maisie said in a far-off voice.

Kate left the subject for now and went up to her room to prepare for the party at Denise's. She was quite looking forward to it — Nick was going to be there.

She wore a blue dress with thin shoulder straps that hugged her slim figure and she felt good in it. Studying her reflection in the mirror, she was surprised at the healthy glow of her skin. The result of working in the garden, she surmised, adding only a touch of eyeshadow and mascara to enhance her eyes and pink lipstick to compliment her lips. Her low-heeled shoes would be more sensible to walk down to Lilac Cottage, but she threw sensibility out of the window and slipped on a pair of high-heeled sandals.

The late summer evening was warm and when Kate arrived at the party, bottle of wine in hand, there were already many people there. Denise greeted her.

'You look stunning. Come and meet Raquel.'

Kate followed her out into the garden. Rachel was a tall, long-legged, raven-haired twenty-something wearing a skimpy red dress and she was holding court with a gaggle of men, Nick included. He nodded in acknowledgement to Kate but didn't make a move towards her. Denise linked Raquel's arm.

'I want you to meet Kate Byron who lives at Kenjarra House.'

'Hi! I had a peep at your house earlier. It would make a fantastic hotel. If you're interested in selling, I know a company who will buy.'

She flashed a wide smile showing perfectly even white teeth.

'Hello. Glad you like the house, but it's not for sale. It's a family house,' Kate said easily.

'But I thought . . . ouch!'

'Sorry, Raquel, did I catch your arm?' Denise said, moving her sister on towards guests who were just arriving.

Kate took a glass of wine from a tray and looked round for a friendly face, not noticing Nick come up behind her.

'You look beautiful,' he whispered in her ear.

She spun round.

'Nick!'

Her face alight, she stared into his twinkling eyes.

'Are you flirting with me?'

'Sure. I always flirt with the most beautiful woman. We're here to enjoy ourselves, so let's make the most of it. OK?'

She laughed, a warm, bubbly sound that caused heads to turn and view the couple who seemed obviously in love.

Frank had fixed up a sound system and dreamy music drifted in the balmy night air. On a makeshift dance floor of rush matting stretched over the smooth lawn, Kate and Nick smooched and held each other close as they danced.

'Happy?' Nick whispered in her ear.

'Incredibly happy,' she murmured.

She was feeling so alive with this wonderful experience, but all too soon, the evening drew to a close and people began leaving. Some friends waylaid Nick, and Kate went in search of Denise and Frank to thank them. On the narrow, wooden veranda that ran the length of the house, Kate saw Raquel sat swinging on a hammock, glass of wine in her hand. She was surprised to see Raquel alone because for most of the evening she had been surrounded by guests.

'Thanks for a lovely evening. I'm looking for Denise and Frank, have you seen them?' Kate asked.

'They're out front.'

She stopped swinging and sat up. She didn't look as radiant as she had at the beginning of the evening.

With no preamble, Raquel launched into her question.

'Are you and Nick an item?'

Startled by the unexpected question, Kate froze. The girl was staring at her. Kate took a deep breath to quell her rapid heartbeat and answered slowly.

'Nick and I are good friends.'

'That's it?'

Kate wanted to say more, much more, but replied, 'Yes.'

Without another word, Raquel jumped up off the hammock and pushed passed Kate.

Kate went and found Denise and Frank. Hugging them both she said,

'It's been a great night.'

Frank put an arm around his wife.

'Glad you could come.'

More guests came to offer their thanks and Kate moved off to find Nick. Voices and laughter drifted in from the darkened garden as Kate slipped out on to the patio. Recognising Nick's voice, she was just about to call his name when she saw a flash of red. Raquel had wound her arms tightly around Nick and was kissing him, and he was offering no resistance.

Kate turned away, to make her way home alone.

7

As soon as possible, Nick disentangled himself from Raquel. The smell of gin on her breath made his head reel.

'Lovely party, great fun,' he said. 'Must dash, heavy day tomorrow. See you around.'

He raced across the garden, aware that, just before Raquel had ensnared him he had caught a glimpse of Kate silhouetted against the lights from the house. Now he must find her, the need within him aching to hold her hand, to walk her home, to kiss her desirable lips. He searched for her, expecting any moment to see her beautiful face with those laughing eyes.

He spied Denise and thanked her for a great party.

'Have you seen Kate?' he asked, trying to sound nonchalant.

'She left about ten minutes ago.'

He headed for home, shoving his hands deep into his trouser pockets, disappointed that she hadn't waited for him. But then why should she? Taking Bramble for his walk before going to bed, he avoided the house, going in the opposite direction.

The next morning, Kate awoke with a throbbing head. Too much indulgence in food and wine last night, she thought, and not used to partying. She took a shower to refresh herself then returned to her room.

She drew back the curtains to reveal a dark grey sky and rain, not soft, gentle rain but heavy, torrential rain and a gusting wind. Her plan to spend the day in the gardens was thwarted. Aimlessly, she glanced around her room wondering how to occupy herself. She didn't want to waste time just hanging around, thinking of Nick with Raquel.

As she sat drinking a black coffee at the kitchen table, she knew there was something she had to do, but her mind was out of gear and just buzzed like a doorbell ringing intermittently. Something needing her attention, but what? Irritated, she voiced her thoughts out loud to Maisie, who was busy at the stove, frying bacon. Maisie gave a quick glance over her shoulder.

'Could it be something of Mr Mansell's?'

Kate pondered a moment.

'I think you could be right. I haven't finished clearing out the bureau.'

'I need to be giving the room a good turn-out. Thought you might like to move into it and have more space,' Maisie commented.

Kate rose from the table. The idea of sleeping in her father's room did not appeal to her.

'I'm quite happy in my room.'

She placed her empty mug on the draining-board.

'I'll make a start now.'

Maisie placed the bacon in a warming dish and said, 'What about your breakfast?'

'I ate too much last night. Let Wilf have my helping.'

Upstairs, sitting at her father's bureau, Kate unlocked it. A feeling of sadness coursed through her. This was so final. Tears ran unheeded down her cheeks as she opened the row of miniature drawers and began emptying their contents.

In the last drawer, something was stuck. She fumbled in her jeans' pocket for a tissue to wipe her eyes so she could see what was causing the problem. Levering her hand into the drawer she drew out a bundle of letters secured with brown tape and labelled in black bold handwriting, FOR MY DAUGHTER, KATHRYN, TO READ.

Stunned by her find she held the letters in her hands and stared at the bundle, her vision blurring. Outside, the rain beat relentlessly against the window, but she didn't hear it.

How long she sat there motionless she was unsure until gradually she forced herself to concentrate on what she had to do. Her hands trembled as she undid the brown tape. The faded envelopes were in stark contrast to the dark, burnished leather inlay as they fanned across the writing flap. All the letters were addressed to her mother, Mrs Violet Mansell. Kate shivered. Goose bumps pricked her arms as she read the first letter written by her father to her mother.

In it, he begged his wife to return home with their daughter. He loved them both dearly and Dorinda meant nothing to him. The affair had been a mistake. All the other letters were unopened and marked, **Return to Sender**. How could her mother have done that, to be so cold and uncaring, and not giving a thought to the feelings of her little daughter? Kate recalled how, in the early years, she had missed her daddy so much.

She opened and read all twenty-five letters. Her father wrote of his love for Violet and Kathryn and of his sadness at not seeing them, missing them terribly. Kate closed her eyes, remembering her mother's bitterness towards her father, not allowing his name to be mentioned.

Consequently, over the years, Kate had believed that her father didn't love her, did not want to see her. Violet had lived a miserable existence, never really happy, and Kate suspected that her father regretted his indiscretion. So why couldn't they have worked out their differences, compromised? It was all such an utter waste of their lives and she had grown up in that overshadow. Maybe that was why her marriage to Vincent had failed, her inability to make a success of intimate relationships.

Angrily, she pushed back her chair. She didn't want to be swallowed by self-pity. Gathering up the letters, she put them into a black plastic bin liner along with bits and pieces no longer relevant to the future. Later, she would throw them on Wilf's bonfire and say goodbye to the past. Somewhere she had heard that the past shapes the future, well, from now on she was going to be in charge of her own destiny.

Hurrying downstairs, she went to the ante-room and found a thick, waterproof coat, pulled on her wellies and set off to brave the rain. She marched along, not thinking in what direction she was going and giving no heed to the muddy paths. Relentlessly she pushed on until a stitch in her side made her stop to catch her breath.

With the sleeve of her coat, she wiped rain away from her face then glanced about. She didn't recognise this part of the estate though through the waving branches of trees she spied the mere. Trudging onwards, approaching the edge of the mere, she noticed amongst tall grasses were the purple flower heads of teasels growing in abundance. They made her think of Aunt Rosemary, a great flower arranger who often used them in her floral displays.

Kate's mind bubbled with an idea. Perhaps next year when the gardens were up and running, Rosemary might be persuaded to give a series of flower-arranging demonstrations.

Without looking, her mind so full of thoughts, she plunged forward to have a closer inspection of the teasels when a male voice bellowed, 'Don't move!'

She tried to turn round but her feet were sinking deeper into boggy mud.

'Quick, grab my stick.'

At the second go she grasped the stick that Harry Leland thrust at her, and gradually, he hauled Kate to safety.

'Thanks, Harry. I'll have to come again when it's drier.'

Seemingly unaware of the danger she had been in, Kate babbled on, telling Harry of her latest idea.

'And I've . . . '

She stopped, seeing Harry's grey face as he leaned heavily on his stick.

'Oh, Harry, I'm sorry. Let's get back to the house.'

'Pocket,' Harry gasped.

Kate put her hand in the deep pocket of Harry's jacket and pulled out a small silver flask. Quickly she unscrewed the top then held it to Harry's trembling lips and he took a great gulp. As the colour came back to his face, Kate offered up a silent prayer. He had given her quite a scare.

'That's better,' he said as he slipped the flask back into his pocket. 'Always keep brandy handy for medicinal purposes. Sorry to frighten you, lass, but you'll have to take more care when you are near the mere. Accidents happen.'

He didn't say, but Kate had the distinct impression he was referring to the drowning of Dorinda. She shuddered, vowing to be more safety conscious in future.

When they arrived back at Kenjarra, an aroma of potatoes and leek soup and freshly-baked bread welcomed them.

'You look two fine specimens and I don't think,' Maisie commented. 'But my mother always used to swear by the goodness of rainwater for shiny hair.'

Harry rubbed his balding head.

'Now yer tell me.'

After quickly towelling dry, they seated at the kitchen table, tucking into the delicious soup and bread. Wilf joined them, but not Nick. Clearing the dishes from the table, Kate peered out of the kitchen window.

'The rain's stopped. I think I'll go down to the gardens.'

Harry, leaning back in his chair, his eyes closed, said, 'Mind you take care. I'll be coming to check on you.'

Casually, Kate asked Maisie if she'd seen Nick.

'He's not been up to the house, but I saw his Land-Rover going down the lane earlier.'

There wasn't much she could do in the gardens for it was far too wet, but she liked to walk around. There was something invigorating about the fragrance of roses after rain. Harry came along and mumbled something about taking cuttings of shrubs to propagate under glass.

'I've such a lot to learn,' Kate said.

She contemplated asking him if she could watch, but he looked weary.

As if reading her mind he said, 'You're best learning from young Nick. He knows all the modern ways.'

No doubt Nick was up to date with the latest techniques of horticulture, but Kate quite fancied learning some skills from Harry before the old ways died out. As she paced the area where the Victorian conservatory was to be built, excitement built up within her, sending adrenaline surging through body and her energy hit a high. George Collins had promised to start work by the middle of the week, weather permitting. She couldn't wait. She headed for the house and to change out of her muddy clothes.

Cutting across the lawn, she was surprised to see Maisie come huffing and puffing towards her.

'Kate, your aunt rang. Can you ring her back as soon as possible? It's urgent.'

Kate ran ahead, leaving Maisie to go

at her own pace. Rosemary was due to fly out to Indonesia in a couple of days and as far as she knew everything was in order, going to plan, unless an unforeseen glitch had materialised. Reaching the house, kicking off her wellies and throwing off her jacket, Kate hurried into the hall and grabbed the phone, punching in her aunt's number. Rosemary answered on the second ring.

'Kate, I don't know what to do. It's Joshua!'

'Joshua!' Kate repeated, stupefied.

'Yes, Mrs Watson, his foster mother, has been rushed into hospital for an emergency operation and Mr Watson is too upset to cope with Joshua. I have him here with me, but I'm flying off on Tuesday. Poor little mite's so miserable. Kate, I'm sorry, I know how you feel about Joshua, but you must come and take care of him until you sort something out.'

Kate stared at the phone, speechless.

'Kate, are you there?'

Kate swallowed hard.

'Yes,' she said, her voice barely audible.

'When will you come?'

Kate told herself she was doing this for Rosemary not Joshua.

'Tomorrow.'

Mechanically, she replaced the phone and padded in her socks to the ante-room and pushed her feet into soft shoes, all the time her mind racing. What to do with Joshua? She would have to contact an agency.

'Cup of tea, Kate?' Maisie called from the kitchen.

At the sight of Kate's concerned look, Maisie exclaimed, 'Bad news?'

Kate slumped on a chair.

'It's a problem to be sorted and because Rosemary's going away I'll have to drive down to Cambridgeshire tomorrow. I shouldn't be gone more than a few days. I want to be back for when George Collins starts on the conservatory.'

She decided not to tell Maisie what

the problem was. She didn't want her new life cluttered up with Vincent's murky past.

Kate didn't sleep very well that night and by sunrise she was on her way south, stopping only the once on the motorway for coffee and toast. She arrived at Aunt Rosemary's cottage just after nine to be welcomed into her aunt's arms.

'My dear girl, you've put on weight. The Yorkshire climate certainly suits you.'

Kate let her aunt fuss over her, enjoying the attention until she said, 'Joshua is still in bed. I thought I'd let him sleep in, give us the chance to talk.'

Rosemary placed a tray laden with tea, muffins and jam on the low table in the sitting-room.

Pouring out the tea she asked, 'Have you come to a decision about Joshua?'

'I'm going to phone round the agencies and find a suitable place for him until Mrs Watson is well enough to have him back.'

Rosemary looked disappointed.

'Forgive me for saying, my dear, but I thought you might have taken him back to stay with you.'

A pained expression crossed Kate's face.

'I couldn't possibly do that. It's unthinkable. Besides, I don't know the boy and he doesn't know me, really.'

'It would be the same with anyone you engaged from an agency. It's not the boy's fault who his parents were.'

Kate stared at her aunt, surprised at her attitude as she went on.

'Kate, it's time to put bitterness behind you. I know you were deceived and that you are grieving, but that little boy has lost both his parents, his foster mother is ill and no-one wants him. How do you think he feels?'

Tears welled up in Kate's eyes. Was she really that heartless?

'I'm hungry,' a small unsure voice interrupted.

Neither of the women had heard the door open. Kate turned to see a tousled-haired little boy wearing scarlet pyjamas, clutching a toy car. Vincent's son!

8

Kate felt a churning sensation in the pit of her stomach, immobilising her. It was Rosemary who spoke.

'Hello, darling. What would you like to eat?'

She took hold of Joshua's hand and they went through to the tiny kitchen, leaving Kate alone, sitting rigid. Gradually, the churning inside began to settle and her mind clicked into gear. Although she was Joshua's legal guardian, physically she had never been involved with him. In fact, she had never even seen him before. How could she care for a child whose very existence she resented? Then her conscience kicked in and Rosemary's words tugged at her heart.

'Coffee?' Rosemary interrupted Kate's dilemma.

Kate looked up, an agonising

expression on her pale face.

'How would a little boy fit in with life at Kenjarra?' she whispered.

Rosemary came and put a comforting arm about Kate's shoulder and said quietly, 'Remember how you hated the very idea of going to Kenjarra? And you were only going to spend the minimal time there. Now can you imagine your life without Kenjarra?'

'No,' she replied.

'And Joshua will only be with you a short time. Will that be so terrible to bear?'

Kate gave a deep sigh.

'You must think I am selfish.'

'No, my dear. In the past year you have had to face up to the deaths of your parents and your husband. In my estimation you are a very strong person.'

Surprised, Kate exclaimed, 'Do you mean it, Aunt Rosemary?'

'Yes, my dear, I do.'

She dropped a kiss on to Kate's forehead.

Kate stayed the night at Rosemary's but not taking any part in the boy's bedtime ritual of bathing and reading a story. In the morning, Rosemary was busy with last-minute packing and she asked Kate to give him his breakfast. Joshua was silent as he ate his cereal. He was trying hard not to cry. Jilly said only babies cried and he was a big boy.

He wanted her here now to cuddle him, like she always did in the mornings, and make him laugh. He looked at the withdrawn face of the woman called Kate as she waited for the toast to pop. She didn't like him, he could feel it. Well, he didn't like her.

'Would you like toast?' the unsmiling Kate asked him.

He shook his head and stared down at his plate and he couldn't stop his tears from splashing into his dish. Kate, concentrating on buttering the toast, wasn't aware of Joshua's plight, not until Rosemary came bustling into the kitchen when his sobs became full blown.

'Oh, my darling.'

She scooped him up into her arms and hugged him close. Helpless, Kate could only watch.

He wouldn't let Kate help him dress or pack his pyjamas, only Rosemary, so Kate took herself off to the village shop. She bought crayons and a colouring book, small cartons of blackcurrant juice, crisps and an assortment of sweets that the shopkeeper said were kiddies' favourites. As she was leaving, she spied a small pair of binoculars, bright yellow, suitable for a little boy. The shopkeeper packed everything neatly into a cardboard box with a fixed lid.

'A sort of lucky-dip box,' he said, handing it over to Kate.

She put the box in the car and went back to the cottage where she found Joshua standing in the hall, his belongings around him. He looked so forlorn, unhappy, his big brown eyes downcast. Her heart did one of its somersaults and she was surprised because she thought that action was only reserved for Nick. She wished he was here with her now.

Then, without hesitation, she crouched down to Joshua's level and said softly, 'Are you ready for the journey now?'

He didn't look at her but nodded.

'There you are, Kate,' Rosemary said, coming into the hall. 'Have a good journey. I've made you a flask of coffee and sandwiches. I'll send you a postcard when I arrive.'

'Have a great holiday, Rosemary.'

Goodbyes were said and eventually Kate set off for home. Home, she thought. She liked that word and she loved her home, Kenjarra. She glanced at Joshua sitting in the passenger seat next to her, quietly occupied with his lucky-dip box contents. Kate breathed a sigh of relief and switched on the cassette player. They stopped at a motorway service station to eat their sandwiches and stretch their legs. Kate rang Maisie on her mobile.

'I'm bringing a little guest with me, Maisie,' she said. 'He'll be staying for a while. Can you fix a bed for him?'

Maisie answered, 'It will have to be something temporary for tonight.'

'I'll leave it to you, 'bye.'

They were sitting at a picnic table and Joshua had his binoculars trained on two birds pecking at crumbs under the next table. His face was alight, relaxed and he laughed. Kate felt reluctant to disturb him.

'Time to go,' she said, and he dutifully climbed down off the bench.

'When we get to Kenjarra, you will be able to see lots of birds.'

As they walked in silence back to the car, a coach party disembarked from their coach. Their chattering buzz of voices surrounded Kate and Joshua and she suddenly felt very lonely. She glanced at the boy and, seeing his solemn face, she slipped her hand into his. He let it stay for a few seconds then pulled it away, so Kate just kept on walking as if nothing had happened.

They arrived at Kenjarra around mid-afternoon. A light breeze swayed the tree branches as Kate drove down the lane and as she caught a glimpse of the mere, her heart lifted. She was home. Joshua sat upright in his seat, craning to see out of the window, his eyes widening as the house came into view. Kate smiled at him. He's going to like it here, she hoped, but his angry words astounded her.

'I don't like it. I want to go home,' he wailed, his lips trembling.

He was frightened. Was he going to be swallowed up by the big house? He slid down into his seat, knocking the contents of his lucky-dip box to the floor.

'Joshua! That's naughty,' Kate admonished.

'Don't care,' he cried.

Much to Kate's relief, Maisie was at the front door to greet them. Opening the car door she spoke to Joshua.

'My, you're a bonny lad.'

She grasped his hand and he hopped out.

'I've some nice lemonade and biscuits waiting for you.'

Amazed, Kate watched as they both went into the house, hand in hand. She followed them into the kitchen.

'What's your name?' she heard Maisie asking.

'Josh.'

'I like that. How old are you?'

Kate answered for him.

'He's three, Maisie.'

Josh pulled a disapproving face, saying indignantly, 'I'm four. It was my birthday last week.'

Maisie threw Kate a puzzled look then said, 'Did you have a party?'

Tears welled up in his eyes and he sniffed.

'No, 'cos Jilly was poorly.'

Maisie clasped him to her ample bosom.

'Never mind, love, I can make you a party. Would you like that?'

His round face lit up with optimism

and he said in a small voice, 'Yes, please.'

Maisie talked about nothing in particular and all the time Kate kept thinking that she should explain about Josh, but she couldn't find the words just yet.

That night, glad to escape Maisie's chatter, Kate slipped into bed. On the far side of the room, nestling in a sofa bed, slept Josh. She listened to the gentle rhythm of his breathing, but intermittently he would murmur out loud, a noise like a sorrowful sob. Tired as she was, she couldn't sleep. She heaved herself from the bed and padded across to Josh and sat on a low chair just gazing at him, her heart full of sadness.

This little boy had no-one and neither had she. They needed each other but she didn't know how to make it happen. That was a terrible admission to make, and for the first time since she was a little girl and her mother had made her say her prayers, Kate prayed.

The next day, Josh clung to Maisie, not moving far from her side.

'He's just settling in, aren't you, love?' Maisie said, glancing uncertainly at Kate.

Last night Wilf had asked his wife, 'Whom does the little lad belong to?'

'She isn't saying, but it's obvious she doesn't know him very well.'

Kate decided, after much deliberation, to confide in Maisie about Josh. The next morning Wilf had taken Josh with him on the trail of repairing broken fences, the ones nearest to the house.

'So if the lad becomes fretful, I can pop him back to you,' he informed Maisie.

And so Kate found Maisie alone in the kitchen, icing a sponge birthday cake for Josh.

'I thought you could invite Denise's two, make it more of a party for him.'

'I already gave her a ring.'

Kate moved aimlessly around the kitchen until Maisie spoke out.

'Kate, for heaven's sake, sit down. You're making me dizzy. Is there something on your mind?'

Kate perched on the edge of a chair.

'There is something I must tell you.'

Maisie, sensing the importance of what Kate would say, put the cake to one side and sat opposite her.

'Go on, lass.'

Kate panicked. No-one, apart from Rosemary and the Watsons, knew the facts about Josh and now it was to become common knowledge, but for Josh's sake it must be out in the open. She swallowed hard.

'Josh, is my late husband's son,' she blurted out.

Maisie looked shocked. Whatever Kate had to say about Josh, she wasn't expecting to hear this and something didn't make sense.

'But who's his mother?'

Kate's fingers strayed to crumbs of biscuits on the table and she crushed them. Her voice low, loaded with hurt, she went on.

'Vincent had an affair with his secretary, and she was Josh's mother. She was killed in the car accident with my husband. Josh survived and he lives with foster parents, but Jilly is in hospital and Sam can't cope at the moment. So I brought Josh here until Jilly recovers.'

'Poor little mite,' Maisie exclaimed, wiping a tear from her eyes. 'And you, Kate, you've been through hell.'

Kate, her pale face drawn, didn't say anything, she just stared into space.

The sound of light running feet and a childish cry broke the stillness of the kitchen.

'Kate, Kate,' Josh called excitedly, bursting into the kitchen.

Surprised that he should call her name she jumped to her feet.

'What is it?'

'Mr Collins is here, and he said I could watch him build. Can I?'

She gazed into his wide, appealing eyes. How could she refuse him?

'Come on, we'll go together.'

Wilf doffed his cap to her as he was coming in and they were on their way out.

'Good little worker is young 'un,' he said with a wink.

George Collins and his two brawny sons, Pete and Ben, were busy unloading materials and equipment. He smiled at Kate.

'See you've brought the foreman with you.'

She laughed.

Josh looked puzzled and Kate explained, 'A foreman makes sure the job is done. He keeps an eye on everything that's being done.'

'Like Bob the Builder?'

'Yes.'

Josh asked endless questions and, always patient, George and his sons answered. They gave him little tasks to perform and with a few bits and pieces he was encouraged to build his own thing. Maisie brought out a flask of tea, fruit juice and sandwiches and Kate and Josh had a picnic sitting in

Kathryn's garden.

'Can I have a garden?' Josh asked as he helped Kate deadhead some flowers.

She glanced at his solemn face. She had such a lot to learn about his life, his likes and dislikes.

'Have you a garden at Jilly's?'

'I've a swing.'

An idea began to form in her mind, but she would have to talk it over with Nick first to see if it was practical. She hadn't seen him since the night of the party, not since she had seen him kissing Raquel.

Later, back at the house, Maisie bathed Josh while Kate had a quick shower in readiness for Josh's belated birthday party. As a birthday treat, Kate was going to take Josh into Burtonsea next day to choose his own present, and then they could take a walk along the seashore.

Maisie had set the birthday tea in the dining-room and festooned it with colourful balloons. As Kate entered, laughter filled the room and she was delighted to see Denise, Holly and Liam. Holly was blowing bubbles and the two boys were trying to burst them.

She met Denise's eyes, full of compassion. She came over to Kate and hugged her.

'Maisie's told me. You're very brave, Kate.'

Kate's eyes filled with tears.

'Don't say any more or I'll cry.'

At that point Maisie came in carrying a tray of her home-made lemonade for the children and wine for Kate and Denise. There were sandwiches, sausages on sticks, fairy buns, ice cream and other delicious party delights. Wilf and Harry came to tuck in and they sang a funny duet together that made the children laugh. Then it was time for the cake, iced blue with Josh written in scarlet and four candles glowing.

'Make a wish, Josh,' Holly sang.

Josh closed his eyes tightly.

'Now blow them out!' Liam shrieked.

Whilst this joviality was in progress,

no-one noticed the tall man enter the room. Kate, laughing, happiness lighting up her whole being, suddenly caught Nick's eyes from across the room.

As if in slow motion, he came across to her saying, 'What am I missing?'

It was Holly who answered him in childish glee.

'It's Josh's birthday. He's Kate's little boy.'

Nick's eyes seemed to bore into Kate and her inside did a double flip, then tensed.

'I'm sorry to intrude,' he replied stiffly, then turning, he strode from the room.

Kate stared bleakly at Nick's retreating figure.

'Oh, well,' she said with a shrug, returning her attention back to Josh. 'Come on,' she enthused. 'Sing happy birthday to Josh'

* * *

The next day, as promised, Kate took Josh into Burtonsea for his birthday treat, though she was surprised when he said he wanted a bag of chips with tomato sauce and to see a fishing boat come in! So, sitting comfortably on the wide sea wall, with their legs dangling, they watched as a huge, heavy tractor carved through the fine sands to the seawater's edge to meet an incoming fishing boat.

One of the crew, well protected in his yellow oilskins, jumped from the boat to couple it up to the tractor. Josh wriggled with excitement as the tractor began to tow the small craft up the incline of the beach and into the compound where the catch of silver, slithering fish was discharged.

'The men are very brave to go out to sea,' Kate remarked, helping Josh down from the wall. 'What shall we do now?'

Josh's long, dark eyelashes fluttered as he concentrated, then he grinned.

'Ice cream, please.'

He jumped up and down, his energy

bounding. Looking at him, Kate felt quite young, like when she was a child. A scant image of two shadowy figures, her parents, flashed across her mind, and then it was gone.

The ice cream was soft and creamy and needed quick licks to stop it from dripping. They stood bare-footed on the soft sand letting the frothy water of the incoming tide swirl around their ankles.

'Fun, fun,' Josh shouted.

'Yes, yes,' Kate echoed.

They raced along the seashore and when breathless flung themselves down on the warm sand to lie flat on their backs gazing up at the cloudless sky. This time last week, she never would have dreamed that she, Kate Byron, would be playing on a beach with Josh Byron. She rolled over to touch his warm arm.

'More?' he asked, springing to his feet.

'Race you to the prom.'

A little later, tired but happy, they were making their way back to the carpark when Kate noticed a couple walking ahead. Their arms were linked and their heads were close together as if sharing an intimate moment and the suggestive laughter of the woman sounded familiar. It was Raquel, Denise's sister and the man was Nick!

Kate's inside gave a funny lurch. The couple stopped beside a sports car and Nick opened the door for Raquel then glanced over his shoulder, in Kate's direction.

She did a quick u-turn, pulling a startled Josh by the hand. She didn't want to speak to Nick or Raquel.

'Kate!' a disbelieving Josh cried as his new toy fell from his grasp to freewheel under a parked car. 'My tractor.'

Shame-faced at her behaviour, Kate dropped to her knees to see if she could retrieve the tractor, but it was happily speeding towards a Land-Rover, Nick's! Eyes down, she ran to intercept the toy and, dropping to her knees, her arms outstretched, it was almost within her reach when she was pipped at the post. A strong, tanned hand clasped the bright green tractor.

'Is this what you are looking for?' a deep voice asked.

Kate jerked her head up to gaze into the twinkling eyes of Nick. But before she could say a word, Josh had thrown himself to the ground down on the Tarmac between them both.

'It's my tractor,' he bawled, not understanding these two grown-ups, whom he thought were going to fight over his toy.

He wrenched it from Nick's hand. Both Nick and Kate looked decidedly sheepish as they rose to their feet.

'Sorry, young man, but I was only rescuing it for you,' Nick said cheerfully.

'It's my birthday present.'

'And how old are you?'

'Four. Kate, can we go home?' he said, pulling her hand.

He sounded fractious and Kate sensed he was tired.

'Thanks,' she said to Nick. 'We must be going.'

He caught her arm.

'Kate, I need to talk to you.'

'I'm not sure.'

She gave a sidewards glance at Josh who was hugging his tractor close.

'Come to my place about eight.'

His eyes pleaded for her to agree.

'Can I do anything to help?'

Not a hair out of place and with skilfully applied make-up, Raquel leaned out of the open window of her car, a bemused expression on her face. Kate, feeling hot and grimy from her romp on the beach, didn't reply. Josh tugged her hand harder.

'Sorry, got to go,' she muttered.

Arriving back at Kenjarra, Josh showed his green tractor to Maisie.

'Wonderful, sweetheart. Now let me take you up for a bath and you can clean your tractor because it's rather grubby, just like you.'

'Maisie, can you sit for me this evening while I go and see Nick? We've things to discuss about the garden.'

She hadn't really intended to go, but

she had this overwhelming feeling, a longing to be in Nick's company, just the two of them, even if it was only to talk about the progress of the garden.

'Of course I can. Happy to.'

Maisie planted a kiss on top of Josh's tousled head. She didn't ask why Nick couldn't come to the house, as it was none of her business.

Kate showered and dressed in a red sweater and cream pants, not practical for Kenjarra but then she didn't want to feel practical. Josh was tucked up in bed with his tractor which he refused to be parted from. Wilf had kindly fixed up an alarm so he and Maisie could hear him if he woke up. Standing for a moment looking down at the sleeping boy, his cheeks pink from the sea air, Kate thought how blessed she was. She didn't want to think about Josh returning to the Watsons now.

Saying goodbye to Maisie, Kate took a slow walk to Nick's place. As she neared the barn, Bramble came bounding down the steps to meet her while

Nick waited in the doorway. Truthfully, she had missed Nick, his friendship. Did she want more? He obviously didn't, content to flirt with different women. And who could blame him after his wife went off with his best friend. She held up her hand in greeting.

'Hi, not too early, am I?'

'No. I wasn't sure if you would come.'

It never occurred to her that he would doubt her coming. She smiled at him and followed him inside, to be welcomed by the glow of a log fire and the delicious smell of sweet apple. She sank down on the sofa and laid her head against a soft cushion, feeling wonderfully relaxed.

'This is a very cosy room,' she remarked as Nick sat on a chair opposite.

'Comfortable, it suits my needs. How are Josh and his green tractor?'

'Fine.'

She sat up. He hadn't asked her

outright what her connection with Josh was, but she knew he was thinking about it. She couldn't bear his agonising so took a deep breath, exhaling slowly.

'Nick, can I talk to you about Josh?'

'Sure.'

She faltered. She wasn't sure where to start. At the beginning, was one of Rosemary's favourite sayings. So be it.

'Remember I told you that my late husband had an affair with his mistress?'

He nodded, his gaze intent on her face.

'Well, they had a son. I didn't know of his existence until the tragic accident. He has no other living relatives so I agreed to be his legal guardian and to be responsible for his upbringing, but I didn't want to see him. The hurt was too raw. Aunt Rosemary was the overseer, arranging for foster parents and dealing with the solicitor and I just signed what was needed. That was it until his foster mother went into hospital and Rosemary is away on holiday.'

Halting, her mouth dry, she gulped, averting her eyes from his face. She heard the swish of leather as he rose from his chair and came over to her, and sat down beside her.

'You and Josh look so natural together,' he said quietly.

His words surprised her and she slowly lifted her head to meet his gaze.

'It's not easy, but I just thought, he's a little boy with no-one and I . . . '

The words wouldn't come, she felt too choked, too full of emotion.

He gently took her in his arms and held her close. He could feel the wetness of her tears on his shirt, the fresh scent of her newly-washed hair as he dropped butterfly kisses on to her head. He desired her so much, this beautiful woman, but she was too vulnerable. His heart overflowed with love for her, wanting to protect her from hurt, but for the time being he must be content to be her friend.

After a while Kate drew away from Nick, feeling a little embarrassed.

'Sorry. May I use your bathroom, please?'

She went up the iron spiral staircase to Nick's tiny bathroom tucked under the eaves to bathe her face in cool water. She glanced at her reflection in the mirror over the porcelain wash-basin. Her eyes were red-rimmed, her face pale and tense. Why couldn't she be more like Raquel, confident with a life not prone to tears? She would go home, feign a headache, which wasn't too far from the truth, but as she descended to the sitting-room the delicious aroma of freshly-percolated coffee filled the air. Nick had laid out numerous sketches on the floor, all full of ideas for plants and seating arrange-ments in the conservatory. Forgetting her recent discomfiture, Kate dropped to her knees on the rug next to Nick.

'My, haven't you been busy? This is wonderful,' she enthused.

'Glad you approve. By the way,

Raquel sends her goodbyes. She's jetted off to Hong Kong to meet up with her boyfriend.'

Kate's eyes widened, but she didn't comment at this sudden, abrupt announcement.

Drinking coffee, they spent a good hour poring over the sketches. They agreed to have hardwood seating, chairs and benches, but Kate was undecided on which plants to leave out.

'They are all so beautiful and yet I know if we have them all it will be too crowded.'

'Why don't I take you into the college where you can see the actual plants in the glasshouses? Then you can make your final choice.'

'What a great idea.'

'We'll fix a date later.'

She stretched her arms then made to get up off the floor, but her legs were numb with sitting on them for too long and she slipped back, laughing. Gallantly Nick took hold of her arms to hoist her up and she was still laughing.

It was so infectious that Nick began to laugh with her. On her feet, she wobbled and fell heavily against his chest, her arms winding around his neck for support.

She felt the gentle pressure of his fingers under her chin as he tilted her face to his. His dark eyes held a longing and she knew in her heart that this wasn't just a passing flirtation. Their lips touched with the passion of two people in love.

Most nights after that, once she had bathed Josh and read him a bedtime story, Kate and Nick would see each other. If he didn't come up to the house, she went to his place or they walked with Bramble. But during the day, Kate and Josh were to be found on site with George and his sons. Kate was careful for them not to get in the way of progress and she often took Josh for woodland walks. Proudly he used his toy yellow binoculars to spy wildlife, though Kate suspected he could see just as much without them, but she was wise not to comment.

On one of these walks, they met Harry.

'How about me taking young 'un under my wing tomorrow? There's something I'd like to show him.'

'Thanks, Harry. That would be fine as I need to see the solicitor.'

Her concern was growing for the unpaid pile of incoming bill and invoices for the upkeep of the house and the garden project. She didn't want to go too far into overdraft and she felt sure there was an unnecessary delay in her father's money being released to her.

Mr Carrick, the solicitor, might not admit to it, but Kate had her suspicions. Without the quick release of the money, the hard landscape work planned for the gardens would be held up and the planting delayed and that would thwart the plans to go for a spring opening of the gardens. She suspected Mr Carrick was bitter because of losing face with the boat club, promising them the land to gain access to the Kenjarra side of the mere. He may be more amiable when he heard her proposition.

On her many walks around Kenjarra mere and when driving into Burtonsea following the road shaped by the contours of the mere, she had noticed a small inlet quite close to Burtonsea. She would offer Mr Carrick access to the mere from this point at a rent to be agreed and subject to planning a landing stage and other facilities. This area wouldn't encroach or spoil Kenjarra, and it would be helpful to have Mr Carrick as an ally when publicising events at Kenjarra. Maybe he could even cajole the boat club into organising a fundraising event or for them to sponsor equipment for a children's play area at Kenjarra.

Kate smiled positively as she entered the reception area of the solicitor's office.

'Mr Carrick can't see you without an appointment,' the young junior said.

In a cool, calculating voice Kate said, 'Please inform Mr Carrick that Mrs Byron wishes to discuss with him a matter to his advantage.'

The girl obeyed and within seconds Kate was ushered into the inner sanctum of the solicitor's office.

9

'How did you do it?' Maisie asked, full of admiration for Kate's business aplomb. 'Solicitors make me nervous, not that I've had many dealings with them.'

Kate related her plan, ending with, 'He looked quite human with a satisfied look on his face when he told me he would call an urgent meeting with the boat club committee.'

What she didn't tell Maisie was that she had to wait three whole days before Mr Carrick telephoned with the good news of the committee's unanimous decision. But the best news was the release of money into the bank so there were now sufficient funds available for the ongoing project of the gardens and grounds.

'Hopefully there will be no more major glitches,' she said, then she added softly, 'I'm determined to have everything up and running by the spring. It will be a fitting memorial to my father, the Christopher Mansell Gardens.'

Just then, Josh ran into the kitchen exclaiming excitedly, 'Look, Kate, a postcard from Jilly.'

He held it up for her to see it was a picture of a family of rabbits.

'What does she say?' he asked excitedly.

'Sit down and we will read it together.'

Seated at the kitchen table, his head close to hers, she began.

'Darling Josh, I hope you are still being a good boy. Jim and I miss you. I am much better now and next week I will be well enough to travel up to see you. Jim and I have some news to tell you. I will ring Kate. Lots of love and kisses, Jilly and Jim.'

Josh bounced off the chair and jigged around the kitchen, singing, 'Jilly and Jim are coming.'

Kate felt her body chill and she

shivered. Maisie gave her a meaningful look, as if to say, are we going to lose him?

On Sunday, Nick rang to ask if she would like to come for a walk with him and Bramble.

'Bring Josh along. I'd like to get to know him better,' he added.

Kate replaced the receiver, visibly moved by Nick's kindness and appreciating his thoughtfulness. But then she felt overcome with sadness at the probable departure of Josh from her life. Legally she knew that she had every right to insist Josh stay with her, but for her, his happiness was paramount. His home was with the Watsons, and his time spent with her at Kenjarra she must regard as just a holiday interlude.

Nick came up to the house to meet them. Kate waited outside the side door holding Josh's hand and on seeing her, Bramble charged excitedly to her, nearly knocking Josh over.

'Heel,' Nick commanded and Bramble

obeyed, but a frightened Josh hid behind Kate clutching at her, sobbing, 'I don't like that dog.'

She couldn't placate him and he stubbornly refused to go for a walk. She looked apologetically at Nick.

'Sorry, another time.'

As she ushered the upset Josh indoors, she glanced over her shoulder to see disappointment etched across Nick's face. She sighed inwardly but while Josh was here, he must be her priority.

Jilly hadn't been forthcoming when she was on the phone about the visit.

'We would rather speak to you and Josh in person. Is it all right if we stay the night?'

They were coming on Friday. If this was to be Josh's last week at Kenjarra she wanted it to be joyful, full of happy memories. To calm him down she suggested watching his favourite cartoon video. So they snuggled down together on the sofa, drinking juice and munching chocolate biscuits.

Later in the evening, she would slip away to see Nick, hoping he understood about Josh's fear of Bramble.

It was after nine when she called to Maisie, 'I'll be about an hour,' and tugged on her jacket and left the house.

Josh had taken a lot of settling. He seemed very fretful and she wondered if he thought she might not let him go back with Jilly and Jim. She tried to soothe him by saying what a nice ride he would have in their car and he would be going home to his own bedroom, for he was still sharing Kate's bedroom with her.

Finally he fell asleep in her arms as she crooned to him songs she half remembered from her childhood and what words she didn't know she made up. She hoped he wasn't sickening for something and the realisation dawned on her that she didn't know anything about his medical history.

Arriving at Nick's, she was surprised to see there were no lights on. The door was locked and her loud knocking went unheeded. She went round to the yard at the back of the old stables. His Land-Rover was missing. Wearily retracing her steps back to the house, she decided on an early night.

When she saw Nick in the gardens next day and mentioned her visit, he replied mysteriously, 'Sorry, but I had business.'

Just then, George called to her and she hurried over to him. Nick went off in the opposite direction.

'How would you like to lay the first brick?'

George grinned, wiping sweat from his broad forehead. The foundations were finished and secure and George was asking her to lay the first brick of the wall to hold the window frames.

'I'd be honoured, George.'

'Where's the little chap?' George asked.

'He's a bit under the weather today so I've left him helping Maisie to bake. But I think I ought to go and rescue her now.'

In the kitchen, Maisie put her finger on her lips. Josh was tucked up on the big comfy chair near the stove that was usually reserved for Wilf.

'Is he ill?' Kate asked anxiously.

Dropping to her knees beside Josh she placed a gentle hand on his brow, but it was cool.

'I think he's fretting,' Maisie said.

'What do you mean?' she whispered.

'Well, from what I can gather from talking to him, he loves being here with you and all of us, but he also loves being with Jilly and Jim. He's worrying that he'll have to make the decision to go or stay, not that he said as much in so many words, but that's how I interpret it.'

Kate tidied the rug around Josh's young body then stood up and turned to Maisie.

'I can't do anything until I know what the Watsons have to say. After lunch, if Josh is feeling OK, I'll take him down to the beach at Burtonsea, and tomorrow I'll organise with Denise for Josh to have tea with Holly and Liam. Then he can play on the swing in their garden.'

Maisie smiled.

'That will be a treat for him.'

The time leading up to the Watsons' arrival was utter physical and mental torture. Each day, Kate was visibly bright and cheerful, happy, laughing, singing, while inside her, misery deepened.

The star of the week was undoubtedly Josh. Children, Kate was learning, have a way of springing back into action. He enjoyed everything and for that Kate's gratitude was overflowing.

On the Thursday, Maisie had packed a huge picnic hamper. Kate, Josh and Denise picked up Holly and Liam from school and were now all heading for the beach at Burtonsea. Nick and Frank had promised to join them after work for a game of rounders. While the sun was still warm, they all took off their shoes and socks for a refreshing paddle in the sea.

Kate held Josh's hand as they ran in and out of the bubbling waves. Then they joined in throwing pebbles skimming across the water to see how many times they would bounce before disappearing. Ravenous, they opened the picnic hamper to sample such tasty delights as melt-in-the-mouth tiny sausage rolls, pinwheel sandwiches of creamy cheese and cress, animal biscuits, home-made lemonade and endless other treats. Afterwards, the children built sandcastles and Kate and Denise watched until Nick and Frank arrived.

Nick glanced up at the sky, remarking, 'We have about an hour of good light for another game of rounders. Josh for our captain?'

Kate nodded, pleased with his suggestion. Once the game was in full swing, the hilarious shouts from the teams attracted quite a few cheering spectators.

Later, as Kate tucked Josh up in bed to read him a story, he flung his arms about her neck.

'Magic day,' he whispered in her ear. 'Can we do it again?'

She held him close, nuzzling her face in his hair, swallowing hard before she could reply.

'Of course, my darling.'

She sat with him, holding his free hand, while in his other hand he clutched his beloved green tractor. In sleep his dark lashes fringed his rosy cheeks and Kate felt the most overwhelming love for the little boy. Tears of joy filled her eyes, tears for the privilege of knowing Josh. She would never be completely ready for him to return to the Watsons, but she vowed never to be out of his life again.

She kissed him gently on the forehead. He gave a sigh and smiled in his sleep as if he was aware of her thoughts.

Downstairs, she found Nick waiting for her with a bottle of her favourite wine.

'Maisie's lit a fire in the sitting-room.'

He slipped a comforting arm about her shoulder.

'Come on.'

Seated on the sofa with Nick next to her, he handed her a glass of wine, saying, 'Here's to the future.'

As they clicked glasses, she looked deep into his warm brown eyes and found herself replying positively, 'To the future!'

After two glasses of wine, she unwound, letting her fears of tomorrow fade for the moment. They discussed the garden and plants, and Kate was showing Nick a gardening magazine when it fell from her hand on to the floor. She bent forward to retrieve it and so did Nick. Their hands touched and she felt the strength of his fingers as they curled around hers.

'Kate,' he whispered and then she was in his arms.

Sensational waves sweeping over her released her passion, her desire for this man whom she loved. His lips were sweet on hers, tender as the morning dew.

'I love you, Kate. I want you to be my wife.'

Was she dreaming?

'Since the day I first saw you and you challenged who I was, you stirred my heart and I fell in love with you, though I didn't appreciate it at the time. I love you, Kate Byron.'

'And I love you, Nick Duvivier, and yes, I'd love to be your wife.'

Then she grinned, remembering their first meeting and how, tired and travel worn, she had not been very polite.

Nick got to his feet, drew the curtains and switched off the lights, leaving only the gentle glow from the fire. He sat down on the rug in front of the fire and held out his arms to her. She moved into his embrace.

* * *

When the Watsons were due, Kate strained her ears to hear the approach of a car. Maisie was busy in the kitchen, while Kate sat reading to Josh. He looked very smart in trousers, T-shirt and gilet and she noticed with a pang how much he had grown in the short time he had been with her. Oh, she cried inwardly, I'm going to miss him growing up.

'They're here,' Maisie called.

Kate thought Josh's face had paled. She took hold of his hand.

'Come on, love. Jilly and Jim are here.'

Jim was opening the car door for Jilly and on seeing Josh, she went to him, arms open wide. Josh was hesitant, so Kate gave him a gentle push and Jilly hugged him and so did Jim. They were younger than Kate expected, perhaps in their late thirties.

'Nice to meet you both. Come on in,' Kate welcomed.

She showed them up to their room.

'I'll leave you to freshen up. Would you like a cup of tea, say in about half an hour?'

'That would be nice,' Jilly said.

'Josh, show Jilly where the bathroom is.'

Kate left the three of them together and went to help Maisie prepare the tea, not that she needed any help but Kate needed to keep occupied.

Later, after they had had refreshments, Kate and Josh took Jilly and Jim on a short walk around the grounds. Jilly soon got tired and Jim appeared anxious about her so they returned to the house, where she quickly recovered.

The nature of Jilly's illness had never been mentioned to Kate and she didn't like to broach the subject. Suddenly the chatter amongst them stopped and Jim gave Jilly a knowing look. She patted the sofa next to her for Josh to sit and she drew him close.

Kate felt her body tense, the beat of her heart quickened, and she felt faint. She sat with a thump on a high-backed chair, glad of its support and waited for Jilly to speak.

'Josh, Jim and I have some wonderful

news. I'm going to have a baby.'

Josh stared at Jilly.

'What kind of baby?' he demanded, his face curious.

She looked to Jim for help. He dropped on one knee to Josh's level.

'You see, little chappie, it's going to be our very own baby and Jilly has to rest quite a lot.'

He faltered and bit on his lip as Josh screwed up his face.

'So you see,' he continued, 'she won't be able to look after you. Maybe when the baby is born you can come and visit.'

'Can I stay with Kate?'

All three looked to Kate. She couldn't see them clearly because her eyes were brimming with tears and her voice was choked.

'Josh, you can stay for ever and ever,' she burst out, and he ran into her open arms.

She swung him round and he shouted with glee. Just then the sound of a commotion came from outside the sitting-room door. Maisie, Wilf, Harry and Nick entered. Nick was carrying a small black and white yelping bundle!

'A puppy!' Josh cried.

Nick put the puppy down on the floor and Josh immediately flung himself down to rub his face in its fur.

'What's it called?' he asked.

Nick replied, 'The puppy is for you, Josh. You choose a name.'

The puppy licked at Josh's face, tickling.

'He's goofy,' Josh laughed.

'Goofy, that sounds a good name,' Nick said.

Josh picked up Goofy to inspect him closer as everybody laughed and the tension passed.

The Watsons went off for Jilly to rest and Josh was proudly showing off Goofy to Holly and Liam who had arrived with Denise in answer to a phone call from Kate.

Kate explained to Nick why the Watsons couldn't have Josh so he was going to be with her permanently. She held her breath thinking he wouldn't want a ready-made family. If that were so she wouldn't blame him if he didn't want to marry her.

Later, once everyone had gone, and leaving Josh with Maisie, they were walking near the mere and Kate thought of her first day, of the silver rippling water and Kenjarra House. Now she had Josh. She should be satisfied and she was, but with Nick her happiness would be complete.

They walked on in silence until Nick stopped, pulling her to a halt, his expression anxious.

'Kate, I want to be a real father to Josh, for him to take my name when we marry. Can I, can we, adopt him?'

'Oh, Nick, yes, yes! I do love you so very, very much. And I'm so lucky to have two wonderful men,' she shouted at the top of her voice, scattering wood pigeons in a nearby tree.

He picked her up bodily and whirled her round until, dizzy, they sank down on to the ground. She reached for him.

Life at Kenjarra, the house by the mere, was full of promise and hope for the future.

THE END

Other titles in the
Linford Romance Library:

THREE TALL TAMARISKS

Christine Briscomb

Joanna Baxter flies from Sydney to run her parents' small farm in the Adelaide Hills while they recover from a road accident. But after crossing swords with Riley Kemp, life is anything but uneventful. Gradually she discovers that Riley's passionate nature and quirky sense of humour are capturing her emotions, but a magical day spent with him on the coast comes to an abrupt end when the elegant Greta intervenes. Did Riley love Greta after all?

SUMMER IN HANOVER SQUARE

Charlotte Grey

The impoverished Margaret Lambart is suddenly flung into all the glitter of the Season in Regency London. Suspected by her godmother's nephew, the influential Marquis St. George, of being merely a common adventuress, she has, nevertheless, a brilliant success, and attracts the attentions of the young Duke of Oxford. However, when the Marquis discovers that Margaret is far from wanting a husband he finds he has to revise his estimate of her true worth.

CONFLICT OF HEARTS

Gillian Kaye

Somerset, at the end of World War I: Daniel Holley, unhappily married to an ailing wife and father of four grown-up children, is attracted to beautiful schoolteacher Harriet Bray, but he knows his love is hopeless. Daniel's only daughter, Amy, who dreams of becoming a milliner and is caught up in her love for young bank clerk John Tottle, looks on as the drama of Daniel and Harriet's fate and happiness gradually unfolds.

THE SOLDIER'S WOMAN

Freda M. Long

When Lieutenant Alain d'Albert was deserted by his girlfriend, a replacement was at hand in the shape of Christina Calvi, whose yearning for respectability through marriage did not quite coincide with her profession as a soldier's woman. Christina's obsessive love for Alain was not returned. The handsome hussar married an heiress and banished the soldier's woman from his life. But Christina was unswerving in the pursuit of her dream and Alain found his resistance weakening . . .